I0626213

BREAKING MEASURES

EMMA RAVELING

Breaking Measures

Copyright © 2015 Emma Raveling

All rights reserved. No part of this book may be reproduced in any form by any electronic or mechanical means including photocopying, recording, or information storage and retrieval without permission in writing from the author.

This is a work of fiction. Names, characters, places, and incidents are products of the author's imagination or are used fictitiously and are not to be construed as real. Any resemblance to actual events, locales, organizations, institutions, or persons, living or dead, is entirely coincidental.

ISBN-13: 978-0-9908847-2-9
ISBN-10: 0990884724

Cover: Damonza
Edited by: Bryon Quertermous

www.emmaraveling.com

First Edition

Printed in the U.S.A

For G
You made it through.

No man remains quite what he was when he recognizes himself.

— Thomas Mann

Something remains in the silence after a performance.

It echoes between the seats, winding through aisles and rows, whispering as it returns to the front of the hall.

The stage remembers.

Its polished floor pulses with the heartbeat of every musician who has crossed it and holds within its infinite memory that which murmurs endlessly in silence.

Power.

The same power pulsating in the thick blood now flowing across the pale wood and pooling around the podium.

This sacred ground siphons away an artist's life, ingesting ambition and arrogance, and devouring countless dreams of immortality so that it can satiate a voracious audience.

The stage demands to be fed.

When you step on it, you become the willing sacrifice.

ONE

The earliest memory Leila Cates had was of her mother telling her to curve her hand. Not her fingers, but the arch of her palm so the row of knuckles would develop into an ideal bridge for a pianist.

She'd started out palming smaller fruits like dates, lemons, and avocados, holding them in the center of her tiny hand between practice sessions, coaxing and molding the fine, pliable muscles between her fingers into absorbing the language of Bach, Beethoven, and Mozart.

When her hand grew and her musical hunger stretched to Chopin, Rachmaninoff, Tchaikovsky, she'd moved on to oranges and apples.

By age twelve, Leila stopped eating fruit. The smell was enough to make her nauseous.

But the repetitive movement stayed, soaked into her muscle memory and as much a part of her as the sickeningly sweet smell of overripe fruit.

Eleven years later, sitting in the offices of Soltano Music International with no piano in sight and nothing to focus on but her manager's sympathetic gaze, Leila reflexively arched her hands, her palms reaching again and again for a solidity long gone.

Her fingertips slid across the sticky leather of the sofa.

"I can't do this," she said.

Joshua Levinson murmured soothing noises and poured more chardonnay into the glass on the table.

"Yes you can, but you need to relax."

Leila reached for the glass, the leather's pebbled texture still clinging to her fingertips, and drank. The cold wine tingled down her parched throat.

"You're just upset right now. If you calm down —"

"How long does it take to calm down after you find out your boyfriend is fucking the concertmaster?"

Joshua winced.

It had been the sounds.

Her boyfriend's low groan rumbling through the apartment's echoing stillness, a woman's soft sighs breathing pleasure. They'd lingered in the air, pulling her to the slightly open door at the end of the hall.

Leila knew she wasn't welcome in Carlo's private atelier, just as he wasn't welcome in her music room.

An artist's domain was private, a haven for practicing and experimenting, the one place where failure was still allowed.

But she'd needed him this morning. It was her day, an important one, and she'd wanted to bask in Carlo's glow, in the way he said her name, the syllables crisply burnished with his Mediterranean accent, his skin warming hers and providing reassurance that her life was right and true and on track.

That was why she'd raced over to his studio just as dawn's pale rays rolled across Broadway and stretched toward the river, picturing his surprise and pleasure at seeing her, the way he would laugh and share in the excitement of her first rehearsal at Lincoln Center.

Her desire to hear his words about making music and love together was why she'd gone there.

But it was her compulsive need to understand sound, to make sense of what each pitch and vibration and tone coloring expressed that drove her down the hall.

She should've stopped.

If she'd walked away, what she'd willfully ignored for months wouldn't now be imprinted in her mind, tangled with countless musical scores and the memories of their three years together.

She wouldn't have seen the way Alexis' pale, slender fingers tightened around Carlo's shoulders while she rode him, the early morning light weaving through her golden hair, bathing her back in an unearthly glow…

Leila put down the glass before it shattered.

Joshua sighed, smelling faintly of deodorant and an expensive aftershave that didn't match his bland, gray suit, and looking like an insurance agent mulling over a claim.

He tapped his foot against the carpeted floor and Leila felt his annoyance.

"It's one more concert."

She shook her head.

"For God's sakes, Leila, do you know how many people would kill to have this performance?"

"Get another conductor and concertmaster."

"This concert has been promoted for the past year. Cates and Belandini. Both you and Carlo are necessary for it to work." He paused. "Did you say anything to him?"

"No, I left."

She didn't want to explain how her voice had disappeared as if melted away by acid, how she'd backed away from that door sucking air through her teeth, each breath stabbing her throat and lungs like hundreds of glass shards.

"Good." Joshua nodded, averted his eyes. "That's good."

His words sank into her. "You knew."

"Excuse me?"

Leila curled her fingers, her nails scraping the leather with a soft rasp. "You knew he was with her."

Joshua straightened the already straight pile of BBC Music magazines on the table. "Carlo is Italian."

He said it as if expecting her approval, a nod or murmur absolving them both of the silent betrayal.

The leather pressed under her short nails. "Were there others?"

"Carlo Belandini is the most important conductor of his generation. He's young —"

"God, Josh, you his manager now, too?"

"— brilliant, temperamental, an original artist —"

"So he can do whatever he wants?"

"As far as you're concerned, yes." His voice turned flat. "You got screwed. You're not the first and you certainly won't be the last. Carlo is irreplaceable. He's the headliner of this concert, not you."

Leila imagined her nails puncturing the leather, tearing into the processed skin and releasing the filling beneath like blood seeping from a wound.

"Your relationship with him played a significant part in the publicity you've received. Most New York debuts don't get this level of attention." The shadow faded from his face. "You couldn't ask for better circumstances."

Her mouth felt dry again. "You can't be serious."

"All that tension makes for great passion." He poured more wine into her glass. "It'll be a memorable night, a concert everyone will talk about for a long time. Isn't that what you want?"

Leila took another long drink.

From the moment her mother sat her at the piano while she was still in diapers, there had been a plan. Years of disciplined training and sacrifices combined with carefully executed steps had finally led to this milestone.

The high-profile concert was billed as a display of glorious Romantic artistry, the blending of Europe's latest superstar with young, American talent, a powerhouse couple ready to take the music world by storm.

But this morning wasn't part of that plan.

"One concert, Leila. Get through it and —"

"And what? Leave him?" Her hand shook slightly. "No conductor will touch me."

Carlo generously rewarded those who went along with his interpretations and ideas and quickly eliminated orchestra members and soloists he deemed difficult. He took things very personally and demanded an absolute loyalty he himself clearly lacked.

Joshua shot her his selling-insurance smile. "I'll make sure that won't happen."

"You can't promise that."

"If it doesn't work with orchestras, then we'll focus on recitals." He furrowed his brow. "Have you looked at the scores I sent you?"

"Not yet," she lied.

Every day, composers inundated SMI with their latest works, hoping to catch the attention of someone on the agency's glittering roster.

In the past, agencies rejected unsolicited scores. But when arts funding dried up and the recording industry collapsed, they'd had to change policies.

Premieres of new works garnered better media attention and could convince a concert organizer to take a chance in booking a newer artist.

Most agents, organizers, and reporters didn't care if that new work was the equivalent of the shitty, forgettable pastels hanging on the walls of countless motel rooms around the world.

But Leila did.

In music, she'd found a perfect language, a way of expressing the inexpressible. Some things couldn't be communicated through words.

Reading amateurish scores rife with clichéd ideas and gimmicks took away her reason for playing in the first place and she resented it.

"All great artists premiered the works of their time."

"I know but —"

"New music festivals are popping up all over the place. You want more concerts? To be an artist that does something relevant and makes a difference?" Joshua spread his arms. "This is how you do it."

His eyes glinted with a hard sheen, the kind of look she'd seen in the eyes of evangelists preaching on television about the glory and nobility found in suffering.

When people first met Joshua, they were usually surprised to find out where he worked. He was only a few years older than Leila and his mild demeanor didn't match up with SMI's aggressive business tactics.

Countless agents were far better at selling their artists than he was and their egos were often as huge as the people they represented.

But Joshua's religion was music and he could sell faith.

In an industry increasingly dominated by the interests of corporate sponsors and frantically competing for relevance in a world of instant gratification and diminishing attention spans, Joshua viewed his job as a calling.

He fervently believed his purpose in life was to bring about another golden age of art by reawakening the public to classical music.

Sometimes Leila wanted to slap him, knock that toothy smile off his face, and remind him he wouldn't have a job if he didn't take his damn fifteen percent off her years of work and sacrifice.

Other times, she liked the idea of him.

Most times, she remembered he was the one who kept her plan on track.

So Leila simply murmured her agreement, reassuring him of the rightness of his zeal and her place alongside his quest to bring the power of live music back to the Internet generation.

The door opened and the chilly January air slipped through, carrying a hint of Chanel perfume.

Marlene Soltano entered, her carefully groomed appearance suddenly making the office look shabby. Thick, honey-colored hair, cut in a fashionable bob, artfully swung around a sharp, angular face pinched with irritation.

"Have you seen my black gloves?" She rubbed her hands together, her voice thick with an accent at the intersection of British, French, and Italian. "I swore I'd left them in my coat pocket but I couldn't find them this morning."

Joshua shot out of his seat, his arms jerking about as if he didn't know what to do with them. First they were by his side, then he crossed them across his chest, and then he dropped them again and shoved his hands into his pockets.

"I haven't. But I can look —"

"No, I'll have Marc run out and get me another pair." She let out a small sigh. "Have you gotten ahold of Dietrich? We need to coordinate programming for Sasha and Natalie."

Joshua dug his hands deeper into his pockets and Leila felt a pang of pity for him.

"He hasn't returned any of my calls yet. I'll try again today —"

"Don't bother." She waved him away. "He doesn't like Americans. I'll call him myself."

Joshua sat, his frame sagging slightly.

She looked at her. "Leila."

The story of Marlene's life had achieved urban legend status. She wasn't born a Soltano, but was the result of her mother's drunken one-night stand with her hair dresser.

Once the infidelity came to light, George Soltano divorced his wife, took custody of Marlene, and raised her as if she were his own. A first-generation Swiss immigrant with a keen business sense and a deep love of music, George founded Soltano Music International with the goal of bringing the world's greatest musicians to the United States.

Despite growing up in a household filled with culture, Marlene demonstrated no passion for the arts and her only interest in music lay in the lifestyle it could afford her.

When George died, her first act as head of SMI was to fire eighty percent of the agents and artists, including some of the most famous names in music. Over the next fifteen years, Marlene rebuilt the boutique agency into a powerful international corporation with an elite reputation and booming profits.

Like most stories musicians shared between vodka shots on a bender, there was no way to know how much of it was true. But it had the effect of making Marlene Soltano one of the most respected and feared figures in the classical music world. She may not have inherited old George's cultural sensitivity, but she possessed an uncanny talent for business.

Marlene considered everyone in SMI expendable and everyone knew it.

Leila stood. "It's been awhile."

"How are you?"

"I'm fine —"

"And your parents?"

Leila felt the familiar tug of resentment. "They're doing well. They're coming in on Thursday."

"From Aspen?"

"Sun Valley."

"All that snow." She gave a mock shudder. "I've never understood how anyone could find skiing pleasant. I assume they'll stay until the opening ceremony?"

Leila nodded.

The ribbon-cutting for the new Cates Performance Arts Center at Columbia University, her parents' alma mater, was scheduled a week after her concert. Leila would perform a few short solo works, while her father smiled too wide for the cameras and her mother stood too close to the senator and mayor.

"It'll be nice to see Paul and Helen again. And I'm looking forward to your concert on Friday," Marlene added as an afterthought. "The Brahms First is one of my favorites."

"She's sounding great," Joshua said.

Leila had forgotten he was still there, something that happened frequently. She supposed that unobtrusiveness was what made him a good manager.

"Is everything well with Carlo?" Marlene asked.

Leila had been with SMI for a year and a half. During that time, she'd gained considerable attention, completed several international tours, and proven herself to be a good addition to the roster.

But Marlene still looked at her as if she weren't sure about her.

She was doing it now, tilting her head, gauging Leila, analyzing whether her talent, her looks, her relationship with Carlo had the marketability to bring in future profits.

A dull ache bloomed behind Leila's forehead, colored by the sparkling chardonnay in the glass, the pleading in Joshua's eyes, and the concert posters arranged in a neat row on the wall behind Marlene.

Carnegie, Lincoln Center, the Musikverein, Suntory Hall. The brilliant colors swam before her, tinted with expectation and the weight of both the past and future.

"We're excited for the performance," she managed to reply.

"And you're in the hall today?"

"Yes."

"Good, good." She looked away, then back again. "The, ah, acoustics can be a little tricky in that space, especially with the heavy orchestration in that concerto."

Leila nodded politely, wondering who told her that. "I'll check it in rehearsal."

Marlene gave a cold, satisfied smile. "Have her new promo shots come in?"

"I was about to show them to her." Joshua pulled a large envelope from his briefcase.

Leila slowly sat on the sofa. Marlene's presence reminded her of what was at stake in a way Joshua's could not.

This was her sold-out New York debut. The *Times* would be there as well as influential presenters from London and Paris.

…his legs tangled in the sheets…

The concert would provide excellent promotion for her upcoming debut recording of the Brahms with the Frankfurt Orchestra.

…her writhing body arched in pleasure, hips grinding…

This was the start of everything she'd worked for —

…and the sounds, oh God, the sounds, each pitch harmonizing with the other in rhythm…

"What do you think?"

Joshua spread half a dozen black and white photos across the table.

Leila's frozen face stared blankly back, her skin pale, eyes overwhelmed by heavy eyeliner, hair pulled up into a severe twist, and body strapped into a gown one size too small.

She looked like a washed out doll.

"They're okay." Her voice was stripped of color.

"They're great," Joshua said. "Like any one in particular?"

She hated them all. "Not really."

"The one on the left makes her look constipated."

Marlene narrowed her eyes and gestured to the last two photos on the right.

"Use these." Her words snapped through the air in a rapid staccato. "Sharpen her jawline and make her cheekbones more prominent. Clean up the hair here and here," she pointed, "and remove that spot under her eye. Was Pablo jet-lagged when he did her make-up?"

"Jeff couldn't get him for the shoot," Joshua told her. "He got someone else —"

"David," Leila said. "His name was David."

"Well, make sure Jeff doesn't work with him again. We need to get rid of those blemishes."

"Sure, Marlene." Joshua's legs jittered. "Sure."

The phone in a back office rang and Marlene left, the air thawing in her wake.

Leila's phone beeped an alert. Rehearsal in 45 minutes.

Joshua glanced at her. "If it weren't for this meeting with the Tanglewood director —"

"I know."

"I'll just have to enjoy your performance on Friday night along with everyone else." He smiled and strode to the door, his eyes filled with renewed purpose, voice deep with the satisfaction of self-certainty.

"Come on, I'll grab you a cab. Midtown traffic is unpredictable."

Leila stared at her photographs, the black and white transforming into strands of notes dancing across the glossy surface.

"Leila. You ready?"

The wine had softened the tension in her arms and momentarily pushed back the sounds of betrayal howling in her ears.

His groans and her sighs now echoed from a distance, far enough she could almost believe they were the last remnants of a bad dream.

"Sure," she said.

There was no other answer to give.

TWO

"So I told him thanks for buying my drink but I wasn't interested." Sayaka Tanigawa, principal cellist of the New York Philharmonic, leaned her hip against the piano, her tall, slender figure buzzing with indignation. "An hour later, the asshole bumps into my hand, knocks my drink over, and says, 'Sorry. Shit happens.' You believe that?"

Leila settled at the piano and rolled her shoulders. She tried not to think about what the empty podium and seat at the front of the violin section could mean.

Sayaka looked at her. "What's wrong?"

Leila ran her fingers lightly over the keys in a quick arpeggio. Blood flowed and muscles stretched. Her cold hands slowly warmed up, figuring out the particular workings of the instrument.

Every piano was different, each with its own set of unique flaws and strengths. The key to making it sing lay in unlocking its voice.

Her fingers flew over the upper and lower registers while she listened and adjusted the weight of her touch, bending the instrument to her will, coaxing the hammers to strike the strings in exactly the right way to produce the sound she wanted.

"Leila."

She paused. "Nothing's wrong."

"You're rehearsing in Lincoln Center for the first time."

"I know."

"What happened to the friend who texted me twenty times last night 'cause she couldn't sleep? Did Josh say something stupid again at your meeting this morning?"

Leila stood and fiddled with the knob to adjust the height of her bench. "Marlene was there."

"Nerves." Sayaka nodded. "Don't worry. Your uber-fabulous lover boy will make sure this concert is the stuff of legends."

Again, Leila wondered why her debut performance hinged upon Carlo.

"I thought he was coming with you." Sayaka craned her neck, peering into the backstage shadows.

Leila wanted to tell her what she'd seen, the nightmare that wasn't a dream, but they were already on stage and the space bound her.

Unlike Sayaka and the other orchestra members who easily chatted about families and late night escapades, Leila was unable to share.

Because beneath the vibrant chatter and the dissonance of tuning strings, she heard another layer of sound.

It was the hum of anticipation, the collective belief that everyone gathered there was about to create something beautiful, something of importance, and it vibrated with the same intensity and zeal as Joshua's hard faith.

Leila listened to it echoing through the empty hall, thinking that if she injured her hands and never made music again, this would be what she would miss the most, the invisible energy thrumming beneath her feet and tingling in the tips of her fingers, the potential of something more than the flat mundaneness of daily life.

This hall was a place of pacts.

The ones she'd made to music and to herself and her parents. The implicit promise made to Joshua, Marlene, her patrons and teachers - and even to Sayaka - to not fuck up this opportunity.

"He was working in his studio until late." Leila forced a smile she hoped exuded confidence. "Probably still studying the score. He'll be here soon."

Sayaka looked like that was what she'd expected to hear. She patted

Leila's arm and returned to her seat, her faith restored and attention already slipping away to matters of more importance.

The air subtly shifted and the buzz of anticipation grew louder.

Just as Marlene Soltano could walk into a room and make everything seem shabbier than it really was, Carlo Belandini made everything look better.

He sauntered onto the stage, the sheer force of his charismatic presence casting a radiant gloss of glamour over anyone and anything in the vicinity.

When Carlo first burst onto the music scene with a first place win at the Milan International Conducting Competition, managers throughout the world had tripped over themselves to get their hands on him.

He made orchestras look and sound better. Strings were more in tune, horns sounded less brassy, the winds soared, music stands gleamed, and musicians glowed with renewed inspiration. Even the stage lights seemed to shine brighter.

Black hair fell attractively over a classically handsome face blessed with a flawless olive complexion and a striking profile. Depending upon the photo, his dark, velvet eyes communicated artistic passion or poetic sensitivity.

A wide smile broke across his face. "*Bellissima*." His mouth lightly brushed her lips. "I missed you."

Leila stared at his hands. This morning, those hands had gripped another woman's hips tight, the nails digging into her skin, his tanned skin a sharp contrast against white sheets.

Now the nails were neatly clipped, the surface buffed to a healthy peach sheen.

At some point between then and now, he'd gotten a manicure.

"We just saw each other yesterday," Leila said dully.

"Much too long for me. Come." He cradled her face with those groomed fingers, polished clean of everything. The soft, moisturized tips felt like acid-soaked spears against her skin. "We make our passion now. Let us fill this hall with our beautiful music."

Alexis Duerr, concertmaster of the orchestra, ambled on to the stage, violin case artfully bouncing against her hip, her chin tilted up, cool gaze surveying the orchestra with equal doses of satisfaction and suspicion.

Carlo pulled away and settled into the high chair on top of the podium.

Alexis stopped a few steps from the piano bench, the stage lights weaving through her golden hair. She raised her brow as if she were surprised to find Leila there, but said nothing while she settled into her seat and unpacked her Guadagnini violin.

Leila sat at the piano, a heavy numbness settling into her arms and shoulders. She feigned paging through her score, her teacher's messy handwritten notes crowding the spaces between lines and cutting through measures in jagged spikes.

According to gossip gleaned from Sayaka, Leila knew most of the orchestra members disliked Alexis, but respected her work as concertmaster.

She was a solid musician, but wasn't a soloist. Despite her preference for flashy outfits, Alexis' artistry was unimaginative and limited. She lacked the conviction to stand alone on stage, preferring to hedge her bets with a group.

Carlo picked up his baton. The buzz of instruments and conversations instantly hushed.

"We'll start with the Brahms." He gestured grandly to Leila. A few musicians, including Sayaka, smiled at her. The rest looked bored. "Then Beethoven and Berlioz."

Leila felt Alexis' presence behind her like a knife stabbing her back. Something cold slithered through the numbness and pooled in her chest.

Carlo stood and lifted his baton.

The lush opening of the concerto rolled over her and Leila closed her eyes, the heaviness in her body soaking up the harmony, the yearning intrinsic to Brahms.

Marlene had been wrong about the hall's acoustics. The rich orchestration flourished in the space, reverberating through every corner with warm clarity.

But something was wrong.

Leila opened her eyes. The strings dragged, drawing the melody out too slowly, until each phrase grew increasingly lethargic, drowning in its own self-indulgence.

Carlo spread his arms, his eyes half-closed, hands slowly caressing the air like a lover.

The orchestra obediently followed him and with every delayed cadence, every extended vibrato, Leila saw the curve of Alexis' naked breasts and heard his muttered Italian words of pleasure.

The piano solo's entrance neared and Leila's pulse quickened, her hands arching and flattening on her lap.

Her turn. Her voice.

Leila played, her fingers drawing the sounds of falling D-minor intervals from the piano at a much faster tempo, her music beating a different pulse, a rhythm far from the images of tangled sheets and exposed skin, from the black and white photos in SMI and the whiff of Marlene's perfume.

She drove the music forward, urging the orchestra to follow her, not Carlo, to listen to her words, her language.

Beside her, she felt Carlo's resistance, his attempts to catch her eye.

The piano's cascade of sounds continued, building to the initial expository cadence and Leila felt a surge of satisfaction as the orchestra left Carlo behind and followed her.

Carlo dropped his arms and the orchestra stopped. Leila deliberately played a few more measures.

"Carina."

She stopped, pulse fluttering wildly beneath her skin like an insect trapped in a jar.

"It's too fast. You're rushing." Carlo tapped his chest. "Follow me, yes? The strings must breathe here."

For a long time to come, Leila would wonder why she said what she did.

But she was tired of waiting.

Waiting for her turn to book concerts, for Marlene to take her more seriously. Tired of reading cheap scores and putting up with bullshit until she was in a position to headline.

She wanted to set her tempo.

And at that precise moment, through the hazy stench of overripe fruit suddenly ghosting over her, she saw Alexis smile.

It was a smile of satisfaction, the same curving of the lips that had accompanied her mewls of pleasure, the purr of a clever woman who'd found a less risky way of obtaining the recognition she wanted.

"It's too slow."

Carlo turned his back to her. "What?"

"There's no purpose or direction." Leila's voice sounded small and rusty. "The music needs to go somewhere. When it's that slow, it sounds bloated and indulgent. Stuck."

Carlo faced her with a patronizing smile.

"Youth." He chuckled as if Leila were twenty years younger than him, rather than seven. A few of the older orchestra musicians laughed with him. "The indicated tempo marking means —"

"Fuck. You."

His smile died.

The hall went mute, the words dampening the vibrations in the air.

Carlo's face turned narrow and haughty, the veil of easygoing charisma melting away to reveal the ambitious mind and calculating narcissism at his core.

Alexis spoke first. "Maestro is right —"

"This is my stage." Carlo's accent turned dark and thick. "In my rehearsal, you do not—"

"You fucking pig."

A hard, ugly knot of anger pounded against Leila's chest but now a hot thread of excitement joined it.

She was really doing this.

She was going with the music, fast and furious, and not waiting her turn, tossing aside rules of professionalism and the Cates family motto of smiles-only in public.

The wild, intoxicating thrill of justice crackled beneath her skin and her arms shook with righteousness. She would expose the truth of the conducting world's golden boy. She would smash that patronizing smile carved into his olive skin and rip the smugness off his face.

"You're a lying piece of shit, Carlo. You're so full of your own crap you can't even tell what's authentic anymore." Her smile widened, stretching her face. "Someday the world will see you're nothing more than a second-rate musician, a child who waves his pointy stick around and expects all the other kids to play along."

Carlo stared at her, his arms frozen in front of him, still gripping his baton as if he could direct the situation.

Sayaka glanced at Leila, her face pale and fragile, then looked away.

"I think maestro is right," Alexis repeated in a louder voice. "It flows better when —"

"Shut up, Alexis." A band of gleeful, giddy triumph stretched taut inside Leila. "Fucking him doesn't make you a good enough musician to understand Brahms."

"I have no idea what —"

"Enough." Carlo lowered his arms, his face adopting the solemn cast of a martyr about to intone his final words.

Only those dark eyes reflected the density of his mind, the way it worked and twisted like a Rubik's cube, figuring out the best way to spin this, spin her.

Because in her haste to shame him, Leila had forgotten the same could be done to her.

"I fought for you to have this concert when most resisted. She's too young, they said. A pianist of questionable talent. Perhaps your charms blinded me and I could not see the truth." He shook his head woefully. "Maybe I underestimated how powerful your family is. But it is clear you do not have the artistic potential I thought you had. You are not ready. This will not work."

The band inside Leila snapped, dissipating the adrenaline in her blood.

A hundred witnesses had just heard Carlo's public verdict. He was the victim, the artist with integrity, while she was nothing more than a spoiled, average pianist.

The orchestra watched her with the same skepticism and distrust with which she'd looked at Alexis. Their probing gazes scoured over her, searching for what Carlo had seen in her in the first place, seeking every flaw in her technique and musicianship.

The coldness in her chest wriggled. Walking away meant accepting their silent judgment. Leila would not concede the stage to them.

She may not have Carlo, or the orchestra, this concert, hell, maybe even a future.

But this space belonged to her.

She remained at the piano, the keys filling her vision, gleaming like a row of white teeth interspersed with gaping black holes.

The grand opening of the concerto once again filled her mind. Leila clung to the majestic harmonies and stately melodic line so she wouldn't drown in the continuing silence.

Carlo gathered his scores and walked off stage.

Alexis murmured something in German, stood, and left.

One by one, the rest of the orchestra followed their maestro and concertmaster, until the last member reluctantly stood and joined her at the piano.

"You're right about the tempo."

Leila nodded stiffly. At sixteen, she'd met Sayaka at a summer music festival. Paired up to perform the Shostakovich Quintet, they'd quickly become close and their friendship had continued through their years at Juilliard.

Sayaka leaned against the piano, holding her cello slightly away from her body.

"He's lucky I didn't shove my bow through his throat."

"That's because it's worth more than your apartment."

And the fact that jobs like this were almost impossible to come by in this business.

She didn't expect Sayaka to jeopardize her position just as Sayaka didn't expect Leila to help her book performances or refer her to an agent in SMI.

Leila was a soloist. Sayaka was not.

This unspoken awareness of musical hierarchy colored every corner of the city, lingering in the corridors of Juilliard, Manhattan School of Music, and Mannes, and drifting like a breeze between music stands, instrument cases, and the open lid of a grand piano.

It hung now between the two women, the understanding that seven years of friendship wasn't enough to risk crossing professional lines.

Sayaka looked away. "Yeah. Doubt my insurance would pay for that."

Leila wanted to tell her how often she wondered what her life would've been like had she simply been allowed to enjoy music, to live without obsessively counting concerts and competition wins.

She wanted to know what it was like to simply be one of a larger ensemble like the orchestra, to have co-workers and a paycheck and a set rehearsal schedule, people you could gossip and share jokes with like any workplace.

She wanted to know what it meant to not dangle in front, alone and separate.

But the stage remained bright and empty and Sayaka shifted, her gaze darting to the others milling about in the shadows, so all Leila said was:

"Go. I'll talk to you later."

THREE

Vladimir Markov loved two things in life: being a pianist and being Russian.

Both were in evidence tonight as he tore into the finale of the Brahms Quintet, his massive Slavic frame hulked over the keyboard, unbridled enthusiasm leaking through the notes.

He played as if he were a young man discovering sex for the first time, uncovering a turn of phrase or a harmonic shift with giddy marvel, the sheer force of his vigor making him appear decades younger.

The Avignon Quartet struggled to keep up, the members' brows furrowed with concentration as his barreling strength pushed them on.

Leila leaned back in the pew, immensely enjoying her former teacher's interpretation, and wishing more people were there to experience it. St. Timothy's Church was three-quarters full, an average crowd for its Monday night concert series.

James Franklin, the quartet's first violinist, pursed his lips, a muscle in his jaw working as a few more notes slipped out of tune, his left hand straining to maintain both speed and precision. Sweat glistened across his high forehead, his complexion a chalky white beneath the harsh lights.

Vladimir took the coda at a heart-stopping clip, the music swirling and building upon itself, and ending in an explosive flourish.

The final chord rang through the cathedral, reverberating for almost a full thirty seconds.

"Bravo!"

Applause boomed. Leila stood, joining the rest of the audience in an enthusiastic ovation that brought the group back for two more encores.

Leila waited until the audience and well-wishers petered out, then exited through the small door behind the choir section into the narrow, dark corridor leading to the back rooms.

The Avignon Quartet passed her, awkwardly squeezing up against the wall with their instruments.

"Nice performance," she said politely.

James shifted his violin case, revealing sweat-stained armpits. "Thanks."

The church's all-purpose break room was where the Ladies Club provided coffee and donuts to parishioners after services and where AA, NA, and every other group with double letters held their meetings. It also served as an impromptu green room for performers.

Vladimir grabbed a plastic red cup from a cabinet in the kitchenette. A frenzied energy gleamed in his eyes, the electricity that had lit up the piano now wildly crackling within him like a downed power line.

He removed a tall Thermos from his bag, poured out a generous amount of vodka, and took a long drink before noticing she was in the room.

"Instrument was shit." His thick, rough accent rolled through her. "Okay acoustics."

"Yeah."

Vladimir once had a brilliant, promising career, immigrating to the United States as a political refugee from the USSR, a celebrated pianist who'd studied under the famed Heinrich Neuhaus and received glowing accolades from Rubenstein, Horowitz, and Richter.

He'd been one of George Soltano's prize artists on the original SMI roster, before Marlene came in and cut him out, along with twenty-five other artists and thirty agents.

Leila wasn't sure why Vladimir no longer had a performance career. Some said it was the Thermos he always kept with him.

But Leila had met enough musicians with intense touring schedules and detrimental addictions to know that couldn't be true. She suspected Vladimir enjoyed teaching, preferring to pass on his extensive knowledge to the next generation rather than commit to a hectic life on the road.

She'd never asked him about it. Despite his occasional flings with female students, Vladimir had kept their relationship strictly in the realm of music, often sharing priceless stories about his years touring Europe or his time at the Moscow Conservatory with her.

Leila didn't want to sully that with talk of business and agents and concert schedules.

He took a seat at the folding table. "How was rehearsal?"

She settled across from him and averted her eyes. "Okay."

He grunted. "Piano?"

"Light action. Wish there was a little more resistance, but it's manageable. Nice treble. Middle range is a dead zone and the bass is a little tricky."

After Leila walked out of rehearsal, she'd shut off her phone, not wanting to hear Joshua's panicked voice or read Sayaka's concerned texts, and spent the early afternoon walking aimlessly in the cold, listening to the constant hum of the city before arriving at the church.

Leila didn't want to think about how she would likely never be able to touch that piano again. She'd come to Vladimir's concert because she wanted to lose herself in someone else's performance, not talk about her own.

"Concert was great," she said.

Vladimir leaned back in his chair. "Yes?"

"Incredible. Quartet couldn't keep up with you in the last movement."

"They play like they're drinking milk," he muttered.

Leila silently agreed.

The Avignon Quartet were typical New York musicians, technically solid with a certain standard of quality.

But it always felt as if they were gigging, not making music.

Their interpretations were superficial, their attempt at depth amounting to nothing more than a cheap, motivational poster composed of trite words and an empty heart. An easy sell, but not meant to be looked at closely.

It was the glistening sheen of professionalism, everything slick and polished, safe and two-dimensional.

The city was full of giggers. Hell, the world was full of them, too.

"I heard James play the Tchaikovsky at Juilliard two years ago," she said slowly.

The quartet's first violinist had made a rare solo appearance with the conservatory's student orchestra. It had been Sayaka's first performance as principal cellist and Leila attended to support her friend.

"I remember."

"You were there?"

"Had to. Fucking faculty." Vladimir took another long drink, the frantic glint in his eyes duller now. "The third movement." He hummed a few passages.

Leila nodded.

"Remember what he did?"

There was a notoriously difficult section in the concerto's finale, a thorny passage full of sharp jumps and tricky intervals that was the curse of every violinist.

Leila closed her eyes, recalling how her pulse had sped up as he'd neared that climax, hearing the swelling support of the strings behind him, and the distinct lack of satisfaction once he reached it.

"He turned away."

James had shifted slightly inward, facing the orchestra rather than the audience, stepping away from the very edge that made it thrilling.

"He flinched, hiding like a coward. Man has no balls." Vladimir clapped his hands, his accent roughening. "To stand on stage means to have arrogance. Faith! You must believe in it."

"In what?"

"In the audience. If you succeed, they will love you like never before. If you fail, the audience will hate you at first. But," he lifted his index finger, "they will still love you because you had the courage to sacrifice yourself for art. Respect, you see. If you play from fear," he shrugged, "you have lost them before you have even begun."

He grabbed another red plastic cup, poured vodka in, and slid it over to her.

"Art exists for the bold, Leila. If you take the easy way out, the stage knows. Understand?"

Leila nodded and drank, the alcohol burning her throat as if sealing another silent pact in a life of too many pacts.

Vladimir exhaled, his face sagging, the folds and grooves etched into his skin now making him seem far older than his sixty-six years.

Leila felt the weight of his life, huge and unwieldy, resting on top of his broad shoulders, stoppering the energy he still had to give.

Part of that weight transferred over to Leila, hammering a weary realization into the base of her skull.

There were thousands of men like Carlo in the world. She could never escape them.

Joshua had been right. If she wanted to keep playing, she needed to get through this performance.

Leila decided to speak to Carlo, tell him what she'd seen this morning and the reason for her behavior at rehearsal. She would be calm and reasonable and explain that her emotions had gotten the best of her.

To Carlo, a woman who challenged his art was someone to be eliminated; but a jealous woman was simply a necessary inconvenience.

Once the concert was over, she would figure out a way of distancing herself with minimal damage.

"Your Brahms," Vladimir said gruffly. "It will be good. Don't worry too much, Leila."

She nodded, her jaw aching from the effort to smile. "Sure."

"When Richter spoke to us in Moscow, he was like a bear with massive paws." The pulsing heat in Vladimir's eyes dimmed. His meaty fingers drummed against the table, playing a memory only he could hear. "The piano was like a toy beneath his hands, but he could play the most delicate Debussy and Schumann."

As Vladimir told the same story he'd told her a dozen times, Leila remembered how she'd remained on stage after the rehearsal, refusing to concede her place at the piano.

Going to Carlo was the right thing to do because she didn't leave.

She'd stayed and shown the faithfulness and guts the stage demanded.

Her hands shook slightly and she took another drink.

Yes, she was doing the right thing.

But boosting her faith with a little liquid courage couldn't hurt.

****

By the time the security guard found them, the darkness outside the windows had deepened and Vladimir could barely stand.

"You two need to leave."

Vladimir chuckled, a dry whisper that skittered against Leila's skin like the way her father's small sighs did when she was younger.

"Larissa," he mumbled.

Vladimir sometimes said his dead wife's name after vodka removed the snapping frenzy in his eyes. He said it simply because he needed to say it, as if her name bounced around his chest and stomach, waiting for the moment it could be freed and enter the world on a soft breath.

Leila turned to the guard. "I called his son a few minutes ago. He should be coming soon."

Once her vision had turned sufficiently bleary, she'd turned her phone back on. The vodka made it easy to ignore any voice and text messages.

The guard nodded. "I'll stay with him until he arrives. You need to go."

"But —"

He shook his head. "Go."

Feeling vaguely ashamed, Leila stood, the ground shifting slightly under her feet, and meandered back to the main chapel. The cheap carpet muffled the sounds of her steps and the rows of pews wavered before her like blurry staff lines.

Her phone's ringtone exploded into the hushed silence and nearly sent her toppling over.

Leila fumbled, hastily pulling her cell out of her purse and answering before she saw the number.

"I just got off the phone with Patricia." Helen Cates' voice jabbed her eardrums. "She said you caused a dreadful scene this morning at rehearsal."

Leila dragged her feet, the phone weighing cold and hard against her ear. She pushed open the doors and gingerly descended the church steps.

"I'm sure she exaggerated. It's fine —"

"How could you possibly think it would be okay to squander your hall rehearsal —"

Leila tripped on the last step. "Sorry," she mumbled, more out of habit than anything else.

"It's just like you to not think before you do something like this…"

Leila squinted and raised her arm, her mother's voice fading into the city lights dancing before her.

A cab pulled over and she climbed in, settling against the sticky seat. "Lincoln Center."

"…you should know that," Helen finished. "And why in the world are you heading to Lincoln Center now?"

"I'm talking to Carlo."

In the week leading up to a concert, Carlo liked to work in the hall at night. It gave him the privacy to perfect the angle that best displayed his chiseled profile, to practice filling the space with his frame, finding the optimal position to command both orchestra and audience.

Despite what had happened at the rehearsal earlier today, Leila knew he would be there. He would never sacrifice his own rituals.

"Well, fix whatever it is you did," Helen said. "I can't believe you behaved in such an appalling manner —"

"Is that all?" Leila leaned back and closed her eyes. The cab rumbled beneath her, eating up the length of city streets.

A long pause. "Have you been drinking?"

"I was with Vladimir." Leila focused on not slurring her words. "He just did the Brahms Quintet with the Avignon—"

"Where?"

"What?"

"Where was the performance?"

"St. Timothy's." The connection crackled and Leila spoke louder. "The one near Wall Street."

Another crackle.

"— suppose even Marlene has her limits —"

"What?"

"—have to go. Norman is here to talk details..." Helen's voice cut in and out. "... your concert's after-party... actually suggested serving shrimp. Can you imagine —"

The line went dead.

Leila had the cab drop her off at the hall's back entrance on 65th, where equipment and instruments were unloaded and hauled inside.

The heavy double doors were unlocked.

She slipped in, her eyes adjusting to the sudden darkness. Using her phone's light, she made her way past boxes, extra chairs, and two concert grand pianos, on to the stage.

A single spotlight illuminated the podium.

Leila's heels tapped a nervous rhythm against the floor, the booming clicks going through her windpipe like a violin bow.

She remembered Vladimir's words - *the stage knows* - and felt its heartbeat beneath her, sensed its breathing, a beast eager to open its maw.

The first time Leila walked away from the stage, she'd almost drowned in the dark.

At sixteen, she'd been the youngest entrant invited to the Chicago International Piano Competition, an honor certain to open important doors for her future.

Her parents had pulled her out of school and shipped her off to Maine, to an isolated, creaky house inherited from some long forgotten distant relative. It sat on a bluff overlooking the sea, a bloated structure whose vacant rooms echoed with lonely hunger.

She'd accepted her exile, understanding that a win at the competition wasn't just for her. It was a win for her parents, for her teacher, for the Cates name. So day and night, light or dark, she'd sat at the piano in the music room overlooking the ocean and practiced.

For two weeks, she'd stayed inside that rambling house like a piece of flesh slowly being digested within its belly.

The night before her flight to Chicago, Leila finally left the confines of its walls. Before she headed back to the never-ending engine of the city and its cacophony of busy lives, before she returned to her world of Beethoven and Rachmaninoff, she wanted a few moments to enjoy the silence.

She'd made her way down the rocky bluff and waded out into the water. But she wasn't an experienced swimmer and an unexpected, powerful undertow had swept her from shore.

As she struggled to keep her head above water, Leila saw the rickety old house balanced on the cliff's edge, moonlight bathing the monstrosity in an ivory spotlight. She'd kept her gaze on it while she waited and waited some more.

The night had been endless, her muscles screaming while she treaded and floated, her body growing heavier as the sea froze her limbs and heart.

The driver sent to pick her up at sunrise enlisted the help of local police when he couldn't find her. They'd rescued her by mid-morning, but it took Helen Cates another three days to pick her up.

Since Leila had missed her opportunity at the competition, her mother had been busy making arrangements for her to play for the judges the following week.

Leila had always gauged her level of fear by that night. She would tell herself nothing could ever compare to the utter shock of that moment, the sudden yank out into the empty dark, the waiting and gasping while the swirling current tumbled around her, attempting to drag her out to the beyond.

And until the moment she saw what awaited her on stage, nothing had.

Carlo lay face down between the piano bench and Alexis' chair, his arms and legs sprawled in an almost cartoonish manner, as if he were attempting to flee both women and had gotten stuck in the space between them.

Beside him was a toppled music stand, one corner stained dark, bits of dark hair and other matter - *tissue, brains* - clinging to the metal.

Leila swayed, spots flashing in front of her, the acrid taste of bile and vodka burning her tongue and threatening to burst from her mouth.

The lights were too bright. Her breathing too loud. The blood too dark.

She wanted to close her eyes and shut out the empty chairs and the stage's heartbeat, shut out the sharp smell of wet pennies - that smell - and the screaming images of Alexis and Carlos, their bodies entwined.

But all she could do was stand, frozen in place, eyes frozen open, frozen like that moonlit night in the water, transfixed by the sight of his blood staining the pale, bleached wood.

Carlo's vibrant olive coloring had drained away leaving behind a ghastly white complexion. All that energy, the barely contained jittery vibrance that seemed to thrash and pound against his chest, the passion he controlled and transmitted through the flick of a baton, was gone.

For the first time, Carlo appeared small.

"Leila? What are you — oh, God!"

Joshua stood in the narrow aisle between the viola and cello sections, eyes wide, skin the same pale beige as the floor, his lanky, salesman figure overwhelmed by the rows of stands and chairs surrounding him.

"What —" His gaze flickered between her and Carlo and his weak chin quivered. "What—" he stepped back. Another. "Leila, what happened?"

"I think he's dead."

Leila heard her voice, a dry, flat *pianissimo* rustling the air like Vladimir's whispery chuckle.

The hall greedily picked up every click of Joshua's cell, spitting the sounds back with razor-sharp clarity.

Leila heard his voice pitched a fourth higher than normal and the words he stuttered to the 9-1-1 operator.

The same serenity she'd felt when the police had pulled her out of the ocean, the air and sun drenching her with warmth and oxygen, washed over her.

Leila recognized it as the crisp, sweet release of freedom.

FOUR

Moving a corpse was no easy matter.

Leila slumped in a seat in the second row, watching cops and CSI and staff from the coroner's office dart across the stage, the buzz of movements and conversations like a horde of insects feasting on blood and flesh.

Joshua leaned over, his face a mask of concern. "Do you need anything? Water? Wine?"

Leila shook her head. The vodka still clouded her mind, keeping the world in a muffled, distant fog.

A balding, middle-aged man, his belly hanging over his belt, crouched awkwardly beside the body, peering at it as if examining bacteria in a petri dish. He poked Carlo's pale flesh with a gloved hand and Leila turned away.

Joshua looked behind him and back at her. "I hate doing this but officers from the NYPD are asking to speak to you. I told them you weren't in any condition to —"

"Oh." Her shoulders felt numb. "Of course."

"You don't have to talk to them now," Joshua fretted.

"It's all right." Leila stood, smoothed her shirt, and tucked a lock of hair behind her ear. With each movement, a small semblance of control returned.

Joshua led the way, his frame humming with anxiety. Two men stood on stage right. The younger one watched her approach, his eyes sharp and bright.

"You the one who found the body?" His voice was low, the words clipped.

Leila nodded.

"Condolences," the older cop said kindly. "Heard you were more than acquaintances?"

"We were involved."

"Gonna have to be more specific," the young cop said.

"He was my boyfriend. We were together for three years."

The older cop murmured vague sounds of sympathy and took out a cheap, spiral-bound notebook. He wasn't as old as she'd first assumed. Early thirties, maybe.

But he wore a sad, dingy suit and there was a general air of defeat to him that made him seem older, as if the job combined with the demands of his three kids and the wife who nagged at him about bills and his health were gradually erasing him away.

"Your name is," he checked his notes, "Leila Cates?"

"Yes, um…officer —"

"Detective." He gave a tired smile. "Ian Brogan. This young gun is my partner, Orion Frazier."

Orion was tall and built like a boxer. Short blonde hair framed an angular face with a strong jaw and eyes the color of the sky on a bitterly cold day. Something furious swirled within their depths, a tornado of cold will and focus.

He reminded Leila of a documentary she'd once seen on Ireland's Cliffs of Moher. The rock formations had withstood the endless expanse of time, forging on despite the constant pressure of erosion, its rugged wildness carving a striking individuality into the coast.

He didn't look a day older than thirty, but Orion's carriage reflected the same unyielding quality as that craggy rock face, as if he'd seen the worst the world had to offer and continued on simply for the satisfaction of telling everyone to fuck off.

Unlike Ian, he'd opted for faded slacks and a dark sweater beneath his coat.

He jutted out his hand. Square palm, bluntly clipped nails. A scattering of faded, white scars covered his thick knuckles. The fine, blonde hair at the base of his fingers were so pale, they appeared almost white.

"Problem?" he asked.

"I —" She wrapped her arms around her stomach and tucked her hands protectively against her ribs. "No problem."

He dropped his hand.

"Musicians have very sensitive fingers, Detective," Joshua answered before Leila could explain. "Their hands are their lives and sometimes people don't realize how painful their grip is. Most of my artists don't shake hands with those they don't know well."

Ian looked mildly impressed. Orion didn't.

"Have you been drinking?"

"Excuse me?"

Orion's brow furrowed. "Have you had any drinks tonight?"

"I attended my former teacher's concert." Leila tried not to sound defensive. "We celebrated afterwards."

"Name?"

"Vladimir Markov."

"How do you spell that?" Ian asked.

Leila told him and he wrote it down.

"He had a concert at St. Timothy's," she added, "and I stayed behind."

"That the church near Ground Zero?" Orion asked.

She nodded.

"And that's where you were?"

She frowned. Didn't she just say that? "Yes. I stayed until around 9:20, then took a cab and got here around 10, I think."

"Alone?" Orion asked.

She nodded.

More scribbling by Ian. "You see anything suspicious when you arrived? Something that seemed out of ordinary?"

She shook her head.

"How did you enter?"

"The back entrance. I knew it'd be unlocked."

Ian paused. "How'd you know that?"

"Carlo always enters..." she caught herself, "always entered the hall the same way as the other instruments because he thought of himself as another instrument of the orchestra. He usually left it unlocked in case anyone needed to see him."

More scribbling.

"Why did you come here?" Orion asked.

"My manager said you needed to speak to me."

"I mean, why did you come to Lincoln Center? Did you have an appointment with the vic?"

"Oh." Leila shook her head. "I wanted to talk to Carlo and I knew he'd be here preparing —"

"What did you want to talk to him about?"

"The upcoming concert."

Orion's disturbingly clear gaze bored into her and Leila concentrated on standing still.

"What'd you do earlier today?" Ian waved his hand. "You know, before..." he glanced at the notepad, "before Markov's concert?"

"Had a meeting with my manager in the morning, then came to the hall for rehearsal." She paused. "After that, I took a walk then headed to the church."

Leila felt Orion's distrust rubbing against her skin. She had the sense he knew everything, including what she hadn't said.

"You argued with the vic at the rehearsal," he said. "What was the argument about?"

"His name was Carlo." She looked at Orion. "Not 'the vic'."

Silence.

"Realize this is difficult, Ms. Cates," Ian said politely. "But anything, even something that don't seem so big, could help us."

She didn't answer.

Orion pulled out a pack of gum from his pocket and popped a piece into his mouth.

Every movement was deliberate. The slower he moved, the more power seemed to collect and simmer beneath his skin.

"Just want your take on what happened," he finally said.

That was when she realized they already knew, that Ian's kind gaze was more than sympathy over Carlo's death, that Orion's unflappable resoluteness was because he'd already made up his mind about who she was.

"I…" Leila hedged. "We disagreed on the tempo for the Brahms."

Orion raised his brow.

"He wanted to perform the piece at a different speed," she explained. "I thought it was too slow."

Ian scribbled in his notebook, the scratch of his pen scraping against the back of Leila's neck.

She wondered if cops like Orion had a bullshit meter, if they adjusted the settings on the dial while questioning someone in the same way Leila adjusted her touch on a piano to coax out its secrets.

"He wanted to perform at a different speed," Ian repeated thoughtfully. He flipped back a few pages in his notes. "Is that why you called him a 'fucking pig'?"

Behind them, a young cop studied a flyer promoting the upcoming concert. The photo of her and Carlo gleamed under the harsh lights.

"Ms. Cates?"

"I was angry," she whispered.

Two staff members from the coroner's office carefully placed his body on a stretcher, leaving behind a prominent stain on the floor.

Carlo would've liked the idea of his blood saturating the stage's wood and permanently becoming a part of this hall.

Leila wondered how much it'd cost to remove it.

A large figure moved in front of her, cutting off her sight line.

"You were angry about something other than speed," Ian prodded. "Isn't that right, Ms. Cates?"

She turned away. "I walked in on Carlo with the concertmaster earlier that morning. I was upset."

Orion shifted. "Walked in meaning?"

"They were together."

"As in —"

"As in rolling around in bed."

Leila's gaze flickered across the empty seats, the flurry of movement on stage, the lumpy shape covered in a white sheet, everywhere but at Orion's implacable face.

Ian consulted his notes again. "This concertmaster the one named Alexis Duerr?"

"Yes." Her voice was colorless.

"Detectives, maybe we could do this another time?" Joshua placed a hand on Leila's arm and she looked down at it, surprised.

Once again, she'd forgotten he was there, hovering along the edges of their conversation.

Orion faced him. "You said the last time you spoke to Carlo was this morning."

Joshua nodded.

"What'd you talk about?"

"Carlo called me after...well, after Leila left rehearsal. He...um," Joshua shot her an apologetic glance, "he wanted to replace her with another soloist."

Leila felt hollow as if Carlo had risen up from the stretcher, stabbed his pointed baton into her stomach, and carved out a hole.

"And you arrived here after Ms. Cates?" Orion said.

"Yes. I received a call from Helen Cates. She said Leila was going to talk to Carlo and wanted me to help her daughter fix whatever had happened between them."

"How did she know that?"

"Excuse me?"

"How did she know Ms. Cates was on her way here—"

"I talked to her." Leila wanted to cover Orion's mouth, stop his relentless questions. "In the cab on my way here."

Orion didn't look at her. "Where were you when the call came in?"

"Having drinks at Fionetto," Joshua said, his smile too thin.

Conveniently located across from Lincoln Center, the Italian cafe was popular with audiences and the hall's staff.

Orion shoved his hands in his pockets. His jaw tightened as he chewed hard on his gum and Leila wondered how long it'd been since he quit smoking. Probably less than two weeks.

"You with anyone?"

"I was having a drink with Charlotte Russell, the hall's programming director." Joshua pulled out a handkerchief, wiped his brow and upper lip. "I rushed over here after Helen called."

Leila had to give her mother credit. Even thousands of miles away in Idaho, she'd still managed to slither into the hall and wrap herself around Leila, Joshua, the NYPD, and Carlo's corpse like a hangman's noose.

The stretcher was gone. Carlo had made his final exit, his life forever defined by the moments he stepped on and off this stage.

"Anyone else with you before Joshua arrived?" Orion asked her.

Leila shook her head. "I told you. I was alone."

The detectives looked at each other.

"I see, Ms. Cates." Orion rocked back on his heels. "I see."

A photographer took rapid-fire shots of the bloodied music stand, the camera's clicks bouncing around the hall like a ricocheting bullet.

Every time the camera flashed and bathed the stage in white light, the dark puddle staining the floor looked like a gaping wound.

****

"The wait wasn't so bad, was it?" Orion entered the interrogation room, file folder in hand.

Ian followed him in and placed a bottle of water in front of Leila. "You must be thirsty."

She resisted the urge to guzzle it. "I still don't understand why I'm here."

Both men sat across from her, one stout and friendly, the other a tall, imposing presence taking up all the air in the room.

The white fluorescent light overhead blazed into her eyes, exacerbating the hangover now drumming against her skull.

Ian gave her a sympathetic smile. "Just wanted to go over a few things, make sure we have all the facts."

Orion opened the folder. "Leila Cates. Twenty-three, graduated from The Juilliard School last year." He paused. "Is it normal for someone who just graduated to perform at Lincoln Center? Thought that place was for old men from Europe."

"I won a competition during my senior year."

Ian peered over Orion's shoulder at the notes in the file. "The New York International Music Competition?"

She nodded. Her mouth felt dry, her tongue swollen. She wondered what else was written in that file.

"Part of the prize was a recording contract and major tour with the New York Philharmonic," she said.

"Headed by Carlo Belandini."

She nodded. "The hall's programming director heard us in Philadelphia and enjoyed the performance so she booked us for a special concert this season at Lincoln Center."

"That would be…" Ian glanced down again. "Charlotte Russell. The one your manager was having drinks with."

"Yes."

Joshua hated Charlotte. When he mentioned having drinks with her, Leila realized how deep the consequences had been for her outburst in rehearsal. He'd probably been begging her not to drop Leila.

"But you were already involved with Mr. Belandini, right?" Orion moved the folder aside and rested his arms on the table. "You said you'd been together for three years."

"We met while I was at Juilliard."

"Was he also a student?" Ian asked.

She shook her head. "Carlo already had a big career. He'd just accepted the principal conductor position with the New York Philharmonic and Juilliard invited him to give a masterclass for students in the conducting department. I wanted to see him teach, so I attended."

"And love bloomed." Ian's smile was wide, overly bright. "Famous Italian conductor and the pretty, up-and-coming American student." He nudged Orion. "Sweet, don't you think?"

Orion remained silent.

"What's it called again?" Ian slouched in his chair and closed his eyes. "That moment when you meet your romantic interest?" He shook his head. "Meet cute, I think. Something like that. Wife tells me these thing but the damn terms keep changing. Hard to keep up."

"You didn't answer my question," Orion said.

Leila shifted in her chair. The walls, their paint yellowed and peeling along the edges, closed in like a set of stained teeth.

"What question?"

"About the concert. I've heard it's a high-profile event with a lot of press involved. Isn't that unusual for someone your age?"

"Isn't it unusual for you to be a detective at your age?"

He didn't even blink. "Not really. Paid my dues to get here."

"So did I."

Ian smiled. Orion didn't.

He looked at her. "This performance with Carlo Belandini is a big deal."

"Every concert in that hall is a big deal —"

"A big deal for you. Your career."

Leila shrugged. "It's my New York debut."

"Important."

"Of course."

"Must be a challenging field." Orion chewed his gum slowly, intently. "A lot of competition in the arts."

She didn't answer.

"Mind me asking when you started playing the piano?" Ian asked.

"I was three," she said.

"Christ," Ian muttered. "My kid's five and we can barely get him to sit at the table to eat. She's been working for twenty years. I've been working since ten this morning and I'm ready to run."

"Must take a lot of determination. Focus. Discipline." Orion tapped his finger against the table. "Ambition."

"No more than what it takes to become a detective by thirty —"

"Twenty-nine." Ian winked. "He doesn't turn thirty for another four months."

Orion didn't acknowledge their exchange. The corners of his mouth tightened and Leila wondered if he ever allowed himself to release that wired energy.

"You list Helen and Paul Cates as your parents." Orion paused. "Any relation to that new Cates building they're putting up in Morningside Heights?"

The headache now drummed a relentless rhythm behind Leila's eyes.

"Yeah," she managed.

Ian whistled.

Leila flexed her hands. "I'm sorry, I don't understand what any of this has to do with what happened —"

"You live on Seventy-fourth and Broadway." Orion studied her, then glanced back at his notes. "Is that The Ansonia?"

She nodded.

"Fancy."

"It's not my place. It's my parents' apartment."

"So you still live at home."

"I work long hours." She looked into those hard eyes. "You think I'd ever be able to find an apartment in the city that allows me to practice on my grand piano for up to eight hours a day?"

"Hell, my downstairs neighbor starts pounding on her ceiling when I wear dress shoes," Ian muttered.

Orion didn't answer, still watching Leila as if she were hiding a knife in her shirt.

"You told us you went to a concert earlier this evening at St. Timothy's."

"You think I didn't?"

"That's not what I said," he said smoothly. "What I want to know is if someone can vouch for the time you left."

Leila remembered Vladimir's glassy eyes, the way he'd retreated into a fog of memories and muttered his wife's name.

Satisfaction flickered across Orion's face.

"The church security guard." Leila willed herself to not point her finger in his face. "I spoke to him as I was leaving."

Ian made a note in the file. "At 9:20."

"Yes. At 9:20."

"And the next time you were seen was at 10:15 in the hall by your manager, Joshua Levinson," Orion said.

Leila waited, her pulse now rhythmically pounding alongside the drums in her skull.

"Thing is, coroner's preliminary finding puts Carlo's time of death between 9:30 and 10 PM." Orion studied her. "Interesting since we don't know where you were during that time."

"I was in a cab."

"You remember something about the driver? The license number?"

Leila strained but couldn't recall anything but a blur of neon city lights and the rumble of the car eating the road beneath her.

"No, but I'm sure you could find the one that picked me up outside St. Timothy's."

"Maybe. Maybe not. Something like that takes time to track down."

"I was on the phone with my mother. You can check my cell records —"

"Doesn't mean anything." Orion leaned back and shrugged. "You could've talked to her right before or after you killed Mr. Belandini."

"That's ridiculous." Leila's voice was tight, as tense as the drum roll rattling her blood. "I had no reason to kill Carlo."

"So you say." Orion rubbed his jaw. "Except for that one tiny reason… what was her name? Alexa? Alexis? And this New York debut. See, I'd be pretty pissed if I caught my significant other screwing around on me a few days before such an important moment in my career. A moment I'd spent my entire life working toward."

"Help us out here, Ms. Cates." Ian held out his hands. "Just tell us what happened and we can —"

"Leila. Ms. Cates sounds like my mother."

"Pretty name," Ian murmured.

"The kind of name that goes with a last name like Cates," Orion added.

"Did I do something to you, Detective?"

"Excuse me?"

"Did I insult you? Do something to upset you?"

Orion rested his elbows on the back of his chair. "Just trying to make sense of what happened."

Leila kept her hands on the table, ignoring the need to rub her eyes and massage her aching head.

"Detective Frazier."

"Yeah?"

"What do you think happened to Carlo?"

"You really want to know what I think?"

She did. "Yes."

Orion leaned back, balancing his chair on its back legs. For about half a minute, he simply looked at her and Leila had the distinct sensation of a storm gathering energy, winds whipping about in his cold eyes, thunder rolling before a lightning strike.

"I see the precious only child of a certain family. I see someone who had it a lot easier than most folks, who probably didn't like seeing her boy toy step out of line right before such an important event. I see someone used to a smooth road suddenly not getting her way and deciding to do something about it."

Leila swallowed the knot blocking her throat. "Why would I do that?"

"You tell me."

"I can't even begin to fathom carrying out something like —"

"Killing someone doesn't have to be planned." He lowered his voice. "It can happen in the heat of the moment. An impulsive decision. What'd he say, Leila? Did he say Alexis was better than you? In music or in bed?"

Ian mumbled a mild objection under his breath but let Orion have free reign.

Leila clenched her hands hard, her short nails cutting into her palms. "You're talking about a crime of passion."

"We won't know for certain until autopsy results come in, of course." Orion snapped forward, the front legs of his chair hitting the floor hard. "Right now, it looks like your boyfriend's head was bashed in by a music stand. Indicates it was a weapon of convenience. The kind of force needed to shove it into his skull would require a lot of anger. Lot of rage."

Leila's stomach churned and she concentrated on holding his gaze, those eyes glaring at her like twin spotlights. It wasn't easy.

"If I'm a young unknown, if this upcoming debut could launch my career, why am I getting all this press?"

Both detectives remained silent.

"It's not because of me," Leila said flatly. "And it's not because of my family. My name only goes so far. I know because my mother has uselessly spent a great deal of time trying to get the media to take an interest in me."

Orion watched her with those sharp eyes, waiting.

"It's because of Carlo. The media has always been fascinated by him and, therefore, interested in his relationship with me. No one knows me —"

"Yet," Orion said. "No one knows you yet."

"Point is, I can't sell the concert on my own. Carlo was the headliner. Why would I take out the very person who could bring me what I'd worked for?"

"Emotions can get the best of us all, Ms. Cates."

She shook her head. "Do you know anything about classical music, Detective?"

"Hell, yeah." He gave a small, hard smile. "Fleetwood Mac, Springsteen, Led Zeppelin."

"Not classic rock." Leila placed her hands on the table, palm side up. "I'm talking about classical instrumental music."

"Can't say I do."

"If you did, you'd know I couldn't have done this."

"How's that?"

"From an early age, musicians build control. We use our hands and fingers to channel what we want to say through our instrument."

Orion studied her. "You saying you don't have the kind of emotion to do this?"

"I'm saying the first thing classical musicians learn is that passion can only work through the filter of control. Emotions can heighten your work if you know when to use it. The art comes before the artist."

She hesitated.

He raised his brow. "Go on."

"Whoever did this wasn't a musician."

"Oh?"

"Performance is about taking calculated risks, finding command in a situation in which so many elements are out of your control. The instrument, the hall, the audience, the weather, even your health or state of mind. It takes years of experience. Practice is about reaching as close to one hundred percent perfection as possible because that means in the actual performance we're likely to hit eighty percent of what we can really do. We work all our lives to have and maintain control. What happened to Carlo shows a distinct *lack* of it. A musician couldn't have done it."

"And yet you did."

"Excuse me?"

"In rehearsal," Orion said. "You lost control."

Leila didn't know how to respond.

There were so many things she didn't understand. Why Carlo had turned to Alexis and lied to her. Why Joshua, Marlene, and Charlotte accepted and excused his actions, but couldn't accept her discomfort with it.

Why she'd said what she did on stage that morning.

"Your job is to achieve flawlessness, Ms. Cates," Orion said quietly. "Mine is to find the flaws. And the first thing we learn on our job is that there are no absolutes. The degree to which people will screw up has no end."

The door opened and a tall Armani-clad figure strode in. "This interview is over."

Ian's mouth parted slightly. "Who the hell are you?"

"Her lawyer." Brian Kensington stood beside Leila and crossed his arms, the subtle scent of money, privilege, and arrogance leaking off his skin.

Ian rubbed his forehead. "Shit. She hasn't even made a call yet —"

"Helen and Paul Cates have retained my services for their daughter. And unless you're charging my client, we're leaving."

One of New York's top criminal attorneys, Brian and his third wife, a vegan lifestyle blogger half his age, frequently attended the same events as her parents.

Rumor was Brian's mother legally changed their surname from Mulligan to Kensington back in the late 70s. She'd read a historical romance novel about a British baron with that name and had wanted to give her son a touch of class.

Leila had only met Brian socially, but she knew enough not to mess with him because beneath the thousand dollar suits, trophy wife, and pompous last name was a neighborhood kid.

Brian had grown up on Staten Island, where family and loyalty were everything and ninety-five percent of the populace were either cops or firefighters.

It was the kind of neighborhood that really disliked people who changed their last name to sound like British aristocracy.

Armed with a fiery temper, a strong right hook, and a fierce inferiority complex, Brian had beaten back his tormentors and kicked a path out, clawing his way to a scholarship at City College and bulldozing his way past the city's countless Ivy League grads to make a name for himself as a ruthless, clever son-of-a-bitch.

Brian was the guy you wanted in your corner because facing him usually meant you already lost. Not only would he come at you hard and win, but he'd also shove your face down in the dirt and hold you there until you sobbed for mercy.

Over the past decade, he'd carved out a career taking on risky, high-profile cases and speaking out on behalf of those he felt hadn't gotten a fair shake.

Becoming the biggest pain-in-the-ass to the very people in law enforcement who'd once tormented him was an added bonus.

Orion looked at her. "Must be nice having parents who can bring in someone like him."

"Come on." Ian spread his arms. "We just need a few more minutes."

"Let's go, Leila," Brian said shortly. "If you pricks even think of breathing on my client again without my presence, you'll have a lot more to worry about than —"

"Don't you have anything to say for yourself?" Orion suddenly leaned in, those eyes cutting straight through her. "You always let others talk for you? Carlo, Joshua, your parents? This ass?"

"Don't answer him, Leil—"

"No." Leila brought her face close enough to catch the clean scent of his soap and skin. "So let me be perfectly clear in case you didn't hear me the first time."

She looked behind him at the two-way mirror, making sure whoever standing behind it saw the truth in her eyes, too.

"I didn't kill Carlo, Detective. Do your job and find out who did."

FIVE

I t took another half-hour of Brian threatening to sue the NYPD for violating Leila's civil rights before they were able to leave the station.

He hailed a cab and waited while she got in. "This is some serious shit."

Orion exited the precinct and leaned against the wall, near a group of cops smoking on the sidewalk. He pulled out another piece of gum and chewed slowly, breathing in the cloud of second-hand smoke, watching them with his shark eyes.

"Leila, you listening?"

"Yeah."

"Every paper in the city is gonna be running Carlo's death tomorrow. You can't pay for this kind of coverage." Brian gave a wide smile, full of teeth. "Tiffany and I will be there."

Leila nodded, uncertain if he was referring to her concert or the ceremony for the new Cates Hall.

He rested his arms on top of the cab. "Want my advice?"

"Sure."

"Helen and Paul will be here soon. That'll deflect attention off you." Brian leaned in, his face sharp and hungry. "Whatever you do, don't talk to the cops again. They might call you, run into you on the street all friendly-like, but they'll turn on you in a second. Don't trust those fuckers. You hear me?"

She nodded.

"Stay inside. Don't answer your phone."

"But —"

"Lock yourself in your apartment. Practice. Meditate. Hell, binge-watch something on the Internet. Lay low until your concert. Once the cops have time to get their heads out of their asses, this will blow over and they'll find another poor schmuck to run down."

He shut the cab door. Behind him, Orion re-entered the station, his stride smooth and long.

Leila closed her eyes and listened to the drumming in her skull, to the commentator bitching about the Knicks on the radio, to the rhythm of life snaking beneath the city.

She got out on 73rd and dragged herself to her building's gated entrance. The grand Beaux Arts architecture alluded to a glorious past, a time when the city brimmed with the promise of artists, rather than the death of them.

"Is it true?"

A shadow separated from the darkness and moved around the corner toward her. Alexis' hands were buried in her pockets, coat pulled tight around her slim frame.

Without her violin case, she was almost unrecognizable.

Leila opened the entrance.

Alexis grabbed her shoulder, spun her around. "Is it true?"

Wisps of flyaway blonde hair flapped against cheeks pink from the cold. Her eyes were a touch too wide, glittering with the pleading desperation of hope.

Leila wondered how long she'd been waiting. "Is what true?"

"Is Carlo really…" she swallowed. "Is he gone?"

Leila registered the subtle scent of something fruity and realized it was Alexis' perfume.

"Who told you?"

"I…" She blinked. "Orchestra manager e-mailed everyone."

Leila remained silent.

Devastation carved into Alexis' face. A wildness entered her eyes, momentarily making her appear savage.

A little less than 24 hours ago, she'd arched in dawn's spidery light, thrust those delicate shoulders back and ground her hips against her lover, reveling in her body's pleasure.

Now her spine curved, shoulders falling forward and chest collapsing inward as she crawled in on herself.

"No." Her voice was pitifully small.

Leila wanted to kick that sunken chest, see how far it would crumble. "Guess you won't get the solo career he promised you after all."

"He didn't do that."

"Did he promise you the Tchaikovsky concerto? The Beethoven?"

She shook her head. "That's not what —"

"You knew it was bullshit. Come on, Alexis. It's not like you have the level —"

"I love him," Alexis whispered, the horror and grief of that realization stark on her face.

Something vicious twisted in Leila and she kicked harder. "I found him, you know."

Alexis shuddered.

"His head was cracked open and his blood was all over the stage. Bits of his brain, too."

She lifted those pale, slim fingers to her trembling mouth. "Stop."

"Maybe it was you," Leila continued, relentless. "Where were you tonight?"

"What?"

"Did you do it, Alexis? Did you smash his skull in with a music stand?"

Alexis stepped back and Leila witnessed the moment love and grief and vulnerability took a backseat to self-preservation.

The flat sheen of focused control she'd told the detectives about replaced the moistness in Alexis' eyes.

"You're sick."

"We all are," Leila said. "You ever thought of that?"

Alexis straightened, lowered her shoulders, stretched her spine. Her mouth thinned until it became nothing more than a slash of haughty disgust.

She walked away, elbows tight by her side, rigid frame disappearing into the city's shadows.

Leila's boots clicked an even rhythm against the lobby's parquet floor. Only after she entered her apartment and locked the door behind her did she allow herself to unclench her fists and swallow the bitterness coating her tongue.

The silent sterility of the space chafed against her skin. She headed into the cavernous kitchen, stainless steel appliances glinting like knives, and took a half-empty carton of leftover fried rice from the refrigerator and a bottle of merlot from the wine rack.

Leaning her hip against the kitchen counter, Leila ate standing up, scrolling through her messages between bites and sips of wine.

Five texts from Joshua, each more frantic than the last.

One message from her mother.

She stared at the notification for a long moment before accessing her voicemail.

Helen Cates spoke with her usual blunt frostiness.

"Those vultures in the press are already calling your father's office. Don't pick up the phone or answer your door. We'll be there Thursday. We can make this work toward your concert promotion, but Columbia doesn't need any negative press before the hall's opening. Listen to Brian and for God's sake, keep your mouth shut."

Leila deleted the message, headed for the master bath, and turned on the shower.

While the water heated, she removed her clothes and stared at herself in the large mirror above the vanity. Within the ornate antique gold frame her mother loved, Leila's figure appeared small and average.

She pulled back her dark, shoulder-length hair and stepped into the shower. Heat and steam loosened her knotted muscles, muting the drumming in her skull and washing away the stench of Carlo's blood and

Alexis' perfume.

Her mother didn't ask if she did it. Neither did Brian.

Leila understood willful ignorance, the need to insulate yourself from the world's shit.

It was far easier to believe your life sucked because someone or something made it so, to believe no consequences existed for your actions and choices, than to take a hard look at your own level of denial.

Helen Cates was perfectly content with not knowing. When her husband went away on one of his countless business trips, she never asked where he was going or why he came home with that slightly manic gleam in his eyes and the rank scent of cigarette, alcohol, and cheap perfume clinging to his shirt collar.

Instead, Helen marched over to Fifth Avenue for one of her own trips, cocooning herself in bags and bags of items she tossed aside the following day, chattering nonstop about Leila's concerts and art and philanthropy so no one could ask her about the things she didn't want to know.

But the not knowing was what kept Leila up at nights.

It was what frightened her that moonlit night in the ocean, the uncertainty of whether her muscles would continue to hold out, the fear of what lay waiting beyond those churning waters.

Do you always let others speak for you?

Orion's words joined the steam fogging the mirror and glass doors.

Leila stepped out of the shower and toweled off, her mind clearer. She couldn't remain locked away, buried in this crypt of an apartment, clinging to lies rather than truth.

She needed to know.

With renewed purpose, Leila returned to the very streets she'd been told to stay away from.

Lamps blazed up and down Broadway, the fuzzy ivory light dancing across asphalt and concrete.

At four in the morning, metal open-weave gates closed over storefronts like shuttered eyes and the streets rang empty. The rumble of early morning delivery trucks wouldn't begin for another thirty minutes.

It was the city's quietest hour.

A buzz emanated from her coat pocket. Leila pulled out her phone, glanced at the familiar number, and answered.

"Hi."

Sayaka's voice was pitched higher than usual. "Leila...can't believe... what..."

The loud music and conversation shrieking in the background drowned out her voice.

Leila crossed Broadway. "Can't hear you."

A muffled clatter, followed by Sayaka swearing.

A few seconds later, she came back on. The noise was gone.

"I'm at a bar with Hector and Katie and it's last call." The edges of her words were dull, softened by tequila. "I just got an e-mail from Patricia Thomas. Is it true? About Carlo?"

"Yeah."

"Oh my God." A few deep breaths. "She said you found him."

With each step, Leila felt her stomach tense in grim anticipation.

"Leila?"

"Yeah," she said. "I found him."

A long silence.

"I'm so sorry." Shock flattened her voice to a dry rasp.

Leila paused on the corner of 82nd. A bright emerald awning graced the entrance of an eight floor building halfway down the block.

The street remained still and undisturbed with no sign of law enforcement.

"Do you need anything?" Sayaka was saying. "I can come over if you want—"

"I have to take care of something."

"Now?"

"They think I did it."

"Did what?"

Leila forced herself to say the words. "They think I killed Carlo."

Another long silence. "Shit."

"I'm going to see what I can find out."

"Wait, what?"

"I'll talk to you later."

"Leila, I don't know if that's a good ide —"

She turned off her phone and strode toward the merry awning winking in the night.

No doorman hovered near the double glass door entrance or in the darkened lobby. Carlo had insisted on a building without one, declaring his studio a sacred space that required privacy.

Leila's legs wobbled. With the same spare key she'd used this morning, she entered the building and took the elevator.

She exited on the sixth floor, her stomach an icy clump of fear, and felt the stale air of the corridor close in. Her hands shook, enough that it took two tries to get the key into the lock and open the door.

A thick silence suffocated the apartment.

Leila turned on the entryway light. On her left, the doors to a closet and a second bedroom remained partially open. To her right was the kitchen.

She made her way down the darkened hallway, carefully avoided looking at the closed door at the back of the apartment, and entered the main living area.

Leila turned on a standing lamp, bathing Carlo's studio in a soft, yellow light.

An elegant cherry wood desk occupied the space in front of a large square window overlooking 82nd. A book on 20th century musicians and another on Bernini's sculptures were neatly stacked to the side.

Next to the books were a pile of scores, topped by a pink Post-It.

Look through these! - M

A hint of impatience marked Marlene's slanted handwriting. Carlo hadn't been immune from the tidal wave of music sent in by composers to SMI offices, either.

Leila rifled through the sheets with distaste, recognizing the same names and signatures on the scores she'd received from Joshua. The pages reeked of desperation.

She turned away. A copy of Debussy's *Prélude à l'après-midi d'un faune* lay open on a rosewood music stand. Custom floor-to-ceiling bookcases lined two walls, the shelves filled with hundreds of scores.

Leila ran her gloved fingers over the spines, some faded and delicate, others new and sturdy. Every musician had their own system for organizing their library. Carlo had used a composer's first name.

She pulled out a slightly worn score for Beethoven's Seventh Symphony, her favorite, and paged through the first movement. An unexpected burst of emotion washed over her at the sight of Carlo's cramped handwritten notes in the margins.

A photo was tucked between the pages of the second movement.

It was of her.

She was asleep, mouth softly parted, naked body tangled within the sheets.

The color and cut of her hair indicated it'd been taken three years ago, around the time she and Carlo had begun their relationship. He'd snapped it without her knowledge.

Leila glanced up at the rows of shelves. The spines that had appeared warm and comforting moments ago, now taunted her.

She pulled out one volume after another, her hands trembling uncontrollably as she flipped through the pages.

Naked photos of other women screamed up at her, their curves and skin and mouths burning into her mind and she felt her knees and wrists liquefy.

Beethoven Fourth: a red-head.

Brahms First: a blonde.

Tchaikovsky: a brunette. Stravinsky: another blonde.

The truth of Carlo's love silently tumbled out.

Once the floor was littered with dozens of images and scores, Leila sat at his desk and stared at two particular photos.

The ground had shifted again into an ocean of unknowns, a dark current yanking at a fundamental law she'd forgotten: there was no truth without a lie.

A soft click shattered the stillness.

Leila stood and peered down the hallway, her skin cold.

The storage closet and door to the second bedroom remained slightly open.

But the deadbolt on the front door was unlocked.

She was certain she'd locked it behind her when she came in.

Leila stepped back, fear clawing her throat. Her ears strained to catch what hid beyond the choking silence.

And then she heard it.

The rustle of something sliding across the hardwood floor.

Her heart hammered a desperate tempo against her ribs.

She could head down the main corridor, past whoever was behind those closed doors, to the front entrance.

Or she could retreat further into the apartment, barricade herself in that closed bedroom, the room where the stench of Carlo's many betrayals saturated the air, call for help and say...what?

That she, a suspect in his murder, who hours ago had been pulled out of interrogation by the city's most notorious criminal attorney, had left the precinct and come here before the cops arrived because she'd wanted to find out the truth?

No. There was only one option.

Leila edged into the hallway and paused.

Silence.

The copper taste of adrenaline flooded her mouth.

She willed herself to move, take another step.

Another.

The front door loomed ahead, the few feet to it a seemingly uncrossable abyss.

Leila broke into a run.

A figure darted out from behind the door on her right.

There was no time to think or move.

Only time to suck in a short, panicked breath.

Leila's head slammed against the wall with an audible crack.

The sound punched through the stifling air, echoing endlessly in her ears as the world dissolved in a howl of pain.

SIX

The hallway blurred, the ground rushing up and dropping away beneath her.

Pain and terror fused into a jumbled mess of synapses firing every nerve ending.

Another shove.

Leila's head snapped back, skull bouncing against the wall a second time.

A shadow flickered along the edge of her vision, striking and pulling away like the ebb and flow of the tides.

Leila staggered forward, arms outstretched.

A flash of movement. Another blow.

Leila's cheek flattened against the wall, her jaw crunching on impact. The invisible assailant locked her arms behind her, applying pressure on the back of her neck until her windpipe closed.

Leila choked, eyes watering, body screaming for oxygen.

Tread. Stay afloat.

Leila squeezed her eyes shut and kicked back. She hit something hard, a bone maybe, and heard a grunt.

The pressure eased.

Leila fell to her knees, coughing violently, blinking through the blurriness.

Her fingers dug into the floor and she dragged herself forward on her stomach, gulping air down her raw, bruised throat.

She stretched her arm, straining for that fuzzy door knob. If she could just reach it, almost, almost…

A powerful hand grabbed her hair and yanked her back.

Sharp pain ripped along her scalp.

Leila opened her mouth, trying to scream, but her body seized and all she could manage was a wheeze, a hoarse cry that rattled like gravel at the bottom of an empty oil drum.

The unknown roared, rising to swallow her whole.

No matter how much she struggled, how much she strained and twisted, she couldn't see her attacker.

But she saw where she was being dragged to.

Her legs slid against the polished floor, unable to gain traction. She wildly flung her arms out, desperately attempting to grab ahold of something, anything.

Pain clouded her head and her hands clenched empty air.

She would not go in there.

She would not let herself be pulled into that room soaked in lies.

The door opened.

Her gloved fingers clawed uselessly at the floor.

Her assailant yanked her hair harder, twisting her head roughly to the side.

Leila froze, terrified of her spine popping, her neck giving way under the force. Something sweet lingered in the air, familiar and nauseating.

Her heart pounded in her ear and her body went cold and heavy. Oh God, oh God, she didn't want to die, didn't want a crude finale like Carlo, with her head bashed in, insides leaking away in a crimson flow.

A thump echoed, far in the distance.

The punishing grip abruptly disappeared.

She heard a soft rasp behind her, then silence.

Leila slumped against the side of the bed. Her cheek brushed the plush comforter and the scent of overly sweet orange blossoms and lilies tickled her nose.

It took her a moment to place the smell.

Alexis' perfume.

Nausea surged and she turned her head to the side and gagged.

"Leila!"

A blistering hot hand touched her arm. In her cold fog of terror, the touch felt relentlessly alive, a fire raging in the winter.

Bright, furious eyes wavered before her.

"Window," she managed.

Orion strode behind her and swore. "Fire escape."

Leila concentrated on breathing. Her skull felt as if a knife had stabbed it in multiple locations. A throbbing pressure ground against her jaw and cheekbone and her shoulders and back felt as if they'd been pulled apart then reassembled wrong.

She needed to get to a piano, sit in front of the familiar keyboard and make sure her arms and fingers could still speak.

Leila tried to stand, then fell back. The room spun wildly.

Orion paced in front of her. "Did you see who it was?"

"No." Her voice was a hoarse whisper.

"Male or female?"

"Don't know."

He glared at her. "Why the fuck are you here?"

Leila ran her tongue over her teeth and slowly opened and closed her mouth a few times. Nothing felt broken or missing.

"I asked —"

"I wanted to say goodbye."

Orion crouched beside her. "Want to try that again?"

Leila dropped her head back on to the soft comforter. Alexis' perfume wafted around her and she swallowed hard against the nausea.

"I wanted to see if there was something I could find."

"Like what?"

She gave a small shrug.

Orion stood, shoved his hands into his pockets and looked down the hallway. "You're not the only one who had that idea."

"What?"

"Let's say I wanted to get rid of something." He strolled around the bedroom, talking softly as if to himself, his shark gaze drifting over the bed, the dresser. "Something I didn't want anyone to find. Cops would go to vic's primary residence first before they found the paperwork on this studio. I'd have time to come in and take it."

Leila shivered. The person who possessed enough rage to shove a metal stand into Carlo's skull had touched her.

Orion stopped. "Again, why the hell are you here?"

"I didn't know I wasn't supposed to come in —"

"I'd advise you cut the bullshit, Ms. Cates," he said quietly. "Because the person who just attempted to smash your face in isn't bullshitting."

Another surge of bile threatened to burst out of her mouth.

"No cops." She coughed. "No crime scene tape."

"How did you get in?"

"Spare key."

Orion exited the bedroom and halted at the edge of the living room.

Leila knew he'd already seen the mess of music and photos before finding her. But she didn't want him to look deeper and grasp the entirety of how little Carlo had felt about her.

She pulled herself into the hallway, ignored the world tilting crazily around her.

"Wait —"

"This is why you came," he said.

She sank against the floor, humiliation joining the aches pummeling her body, too damn tired to deny it.

Orion removed a pen from his coat pocket and used it to push aside scores, examining the bizarre scrapbook of photos and symphonic orchestrations.

"You touch any of this?"

Leila shook her head, wincing as pain shimmied across her skull. She slowly lifted her gloved hands.

Orion looked at them, then back at the mess on the floor. Silent, he edged his way around to the desk in front of the window.

Leila closed her eyes, seeing in her mind the two photos Orion now studied, the images as indelible as those of Carlo and Alexis in the bed behind her.

"You know these two?"

At that moment, Leila realized she'd possessed the same warped belief as Joshua and Vladimir.

She'd devoutly believed in the trajectory of her life, in Carlo, in the fabulous narrative of their relationship and intertwined careers.

But reality was always so much more pedestrian than dreams.

Leila opened her eyes to find the detective studying her.

"One on the left," she croaked, "is the head of SMI, my agency. Name's Marlene Soltano. She was Carlo's manager."

Orion turned back to the desk. "And the one on the right?"

"Sayaka Tanikawa." Leila's voice cracked slightly. She cleared her throat. "Principal cellist with the New York Philharmonic."

"The one Carlo led?"

"Yeah."

He turned to look at her.

"A friend."

For a full minute, Marlene and Sayaka's sprawling naked bodies flashed between them like the garish glow of neon lights.

Leila wondered how many images her mother carried around in her head and what it took to make them go away.

"Guessing you found one of yours, too," he finally said.

"I'm not giving it to you."

"You realize that's obstruction of justice."

"Give me a break —"

"Looks real suspicious if your photo is the only one missing. People will wonder if someone came and took it."

"But —"

He raised his hand. "Next obvious question would be what else that person may have to hide."

Leila exhaled.

She gingerly removed the photo she'd shoved deep into her coat pocket and handed it to him, image side down.

Orion pulled the sleeve of his coat over his hand and placed the photo on the ground without looking at it.

"We need to go," he said tersely. "My guys will be here soon."

We. He wasn't bringing her in.

"You don't think it was me."

He glanced at the front door.

"Then why did you interrogate —"

"Ms. Cates. We're leaving here together and then you're going to answer a few more questions."

That was the last thing she wanted.

But answering the stubborn detective's questions was still better than staying here, where fruity scents scorched her nose and pages of music concealed rotting secrets.

"Can you walk?"

She gave a small nod.

Orion helped her off the ground and they left, closing the door behind them, cutting Leila off from a life she'd once believed in.

She was now afloat, faithless and alone, without an anchor or purpose.

The city had passed its sleeping hour and restarted for a new day. Warm air from the subway drifted through the grates in the sidewalk. A young man, bundled in layers of clothing, delivered stacks of the day's papers to the corner kiosk. A bagel shop employee rolled open the gate covering his storefront.

It wasn't until they'd walked for a few blocks that Leila realized Orion's grip when he helped her up had been firm but gentle, as if careful to not injure her fingers.

****

The gilded edges of the antique, ornate mirror above the vanity now framed a very different face.

Leila's jaw was already swollen, the flesh turning a vicious purple. Her teeth were in tact, but pain lanced through her cheekbones each time she opened her mouth.

She carefully rubbed pain-relieving cream into her shoulders and upper back, the icy hot sting easing her battered muscles, then left to deal with the detective in her apartment.

Leila found Orion in the kitchen, peering into the freezer.

"You don't have frozen vegetables."

"What?"

He pulled back and shut the door.

"There's nothing in your freezer. If you didn't have an ice machine, you wouldn't even have ice."

"I don't use this kitchen much."

"Did you take pain killers? Ibuprofen?"

"No."

"Why not?"

"Don't have any. Never needed it before."

Orion frowned and handed over a towel wrapped around ice cubes.

She awkwardly pressed it against her shoulder.

"No." He nodded at her left cheek. "Here."

Leila placed the towel against her jaw and let out a hiss of pain.

Orion strode down the hallway, his confident movements indicating he'd checked out the apartment while she'd been in the bathroom.

Leila followed him into the music room and placed the towel in the large, brightly colored centerpiece bowl on the coffee table. The cold bothered her hand.

Orion stood before a shelf lined with photos. All featured her parents posing with a variety of politicians and CEOs.

One photo of Leila lay nestled among the dozens featuring Helen and Paul Cates. It was taken during her debut performance with the Orchestre de Paris.

A fresh-faced eighteen-year-old just out of high school, she'd clinched the concert by winning the grand prize in her first major international competition.

Leila had performed that night believing in her destiny.

The win had validated the rightness of her life and justified the endless days and nights of lonely doubts.

Orion picked up that photo, effortlessly finding it among the others.

The longer he studied it, the more vulnerable Leila felt.

She suddenly saw the image through his eyes: the dress clinging to her thin frame, a carefully constructed confection binding her tight, making her appear both feminine and sexual like a child puppet manipulated by invisible strings.

She saw the overly bright lights, the harsh stain of her lipstick, the practiced grand gestures of the conductor, the boredom etched onto the faces of the older musicians in the orchestra, irritated at accompanying a child.

Leila didn't want him to see her that way.

"Can I take your coat?" she asked.

Orion's mouth tightened as if he found the question rude rather than polite. He returned the photo to the shelf, removed his coat, and handed it over.

The sleeve of his shirt caught above his elbow, revealing his right forearm.

Beneath the fine blonde hair was a network of ugly raised scars. They wound up from wrist to elbow, the jagged lines carved with the same intensity reflected in his eyes.

Orion jerked, hastily yanking the sleeve down.

Leila walked away, pretending nothing had happened, and hung his coat in the entry closet. She also grabbed the half-empty bottle of merlot she'd had with dinner and two glasses.

When she returned, Orion had already taken a seat on the sofa.

Leila settled across from him and placed the bottle on the table beside the bright bowl.

"You were lucky," he said tersely.

"I think my face disagrees."

"It'll keep swelling if you don't put ice on it."

"I'll do it later." She poured herself a glass of wine. "Would you like some?"

"No."

Leila drank, feeling the alcohol numb the pain and her frayed nerves, avoiding his unrelenting gaze.

She cleared her throat. "Thank you for... you know, getting me out —"

"You shouldn't have been there."

"No one told me not to go."

Orion studied her for a moment, then gestured at the Steinway grand tucked into the corner. "What were you playing earlier?"

"Brahms."

Upon returning home, Leila had immediately settled at the piano and was relieved to discover the ache in her shoulders and back hadn't affected her arms or fingers.

"Is that what you're performing on Friday?" His voice was rough with exhaustion, his accent more pronounced.

"Yes. Did you like it?"

Orion shrugged. "Sounded like a bunch of notes."

Leila knew he didn't like or understand her music. But she still felt disappointed that he hadn't heard more in it.

"Was your father a cop, too?" she asked.

A pause. "No."

She tried again, this time with a statement rather than a question.

"You're from Long Island."

"Born and raised." He nodded at a triangular-shaped object on the side table beside the piano. "I've seen something like that at a friend's house. What is it?"

"A metronome."

Leila had found it a tiny store in Milan a few years ago.

She gently pushed the pendulum and it swung back and forth with a smooth, even movement, the measured beats ticking like a loud clock.

She nudged the adjustable weight down to *presto*. The metronome swung faster, a rapid beat pulsing with electric energy.

"It provides a reference for different speeds in music."

"Tempo," Orion said.

She nodded, surprised he'd remembered.

"Do you use it?

"Sometimes, if I want to double-check something." She traced the *fleur de lis* etched into the rosewood base. "But most musicians have already internalized them."

The same constriction Leila felt during her last rehearsal with Carlo clamped around her chest.

The very rules that defined her music, the boundaries that gave her art meaning and her life purpose, suddenly felt absurd.

Why did an *allegretto* have to be between 112-120 beats per minute? Or a *lento* between 45-60 beats per minute?

Leila stopped the metronome's swinging rod and the sudden silence thudded against the walls.

"You said you had questions for me."

Orion leaned back, stretched his arms across the back of the sofa. "You grew up here?"

A faint note of tension entered his voice. Not disapproval exactly, but a sliver of irritation from rubbing against something distasteful.

Leila heard the same pitch when a grocery store cashier gave change to an impatient Wall Street banker or when her father said "those people" to refer to anyone with less than a high six-figure income.

"I think of New York as home but I traveled a lot from an early age to study with different teachers in Europe, Asia, Russia."

"What about outside of music? Did you go to boarding school or something?"

"Mostly private tutors."

He shifted again, his frame dwarfing the low, minimalist sofa. "Hell of a way to grow up."

"It's not real."

Orion waited for her to continue.

"All of this." Leila gestured at the paintings, the hard, cold furnishings, the photos and accouterments, everything placed just so.

"It's your family. Your home."

Leila shook her head. "It's an investment. Acquired assets, protected and developed for future gains."

"Including you?"

"Yes." She tilted her chin, daring him to say otherwise.

But he simply asked, "What happens if there's no return?"

"That's not an option."

Something flickered through his eyes, an awareness that suddenly left Leila feeling empty.

She didn't want to talk about a life she no longer understood. This week was supposed to follow a well-laid track.

Instead, here she sat, across from a NYPD detective, her face swollen, her insides a ragged mess, with no plan for how to proceed.

She needed to understand what broke the path.

"Have you found anything new?"

Orion raised his brow. "In the few hours since you left the station?"

She flushed. "I thought maybe —"

"You have to stop what you're doing."

Leila took another drink. With each passing second, a tipsy recklessness emboldened her.

"Is that a warning?"

"I'm not the one you need to be worried about."

"I'm not a threat. To anyone."

There was too much truth in that statement, more than she intended to say.

She met his plaintive glare. "I need to know."

"It's not going to bring him back."

A bark of laughter escaped her lips. "Is that what you think I'm doing?"

"He's dead."

"No shit."

"You'll never be able to change what happened. What he did."

Leila placed the wine glass on the table, concentrating on keeping her hand steady.

"You'll never make him understand that you see him for the lying prick he is," he continued flatly. "You'll never make him bleed and suffer for what he did or have the satisfaction of kicking him to the curb or find out why he did any of it. You'll never have the closure you want because he's not coming back — "

"I *know*."

He stopped.

Leila's throat closed up and she waited for the flood of emotion to subside. She wouldn't cry. Not in front of him.

"Why are you doing this?"

Orion leaned forward, balanced his elbows on his knees. "Carlo seems like the kind of person who'd piss off quite a few people. To find out who did this, I need to know what drove your boyfriend." He paused. "What drives you."

"But why —" She stopped. "You still think a musician did it."

He gave a short nod.

Leila disagreed with his assessment, but she accepted his explanation.

Her world was his unknown and he needed to understand.

"What do you want to know?"

"Why do this? All those years of training and practice, sacrificing your childhood, your life to pursue something with this level of dedication?"

"What drives any performer?" She looked at him. "Athletes? Actors? Dancers?"

Most people offered cheap answers: money, fame, vanity, or the glory of the win.

Orion didn't. "Achievement."

Leila nodded. "The desire to be remembered."

"And validated," he added.

The same need that drove people to achieve also drove them to have kids.

It was the fundamental human desire to live forever, whether it was through achievement or genetic makeup, ensuring some part of them would still remain after death in the same way Carlo's blood had permanently seeped into the stage.

Leaving something behind - a child, a business, a staggering medical discovery, a memorable performance or recording - provided reassurance to people that their lives weren't just tiny, irrelevant blips on the radar of human civilization, but had *meant* something.

Leila thought of her parents, attaching the Cates name to endowments and scholarships and buildings as if using a label maker.

She looked at him. "Creating a legacy is a way of ensuring immortality."

"Protecting that would be worth killing for."

"Doesn't mean the killer's a musician."

"Doesn't mean he's not."

"There was a concert earlier tonight in the hall, right? The Manhattan Chamber Ensemble?"

Despite the number of musicians in the city, the artistic community was small. Several of Leila's former classmates from Juilliard were in the ensemble and had e-mailed her info about the performance.

Orion nodded. "Started at 7:30. Ended around 9:15."

"Someone could've entered the hall after the concert ended. Before or after Carlo arrived," Leila pressed. "Is there a way to check?"

He waited a beat. "We took a look at camera footage covering the back entrance."

"And?"

"Dozens of people went in and out. Musicians, stage crew, audience. It'll take time to sort through all of them."

Outside the window, the night had lightened to a pale blue. Dawn's pink threads wove through the sky like fine veins carrying the promise of a new day.

Leila remembered the crowd of people buzzing around Carlo's body, the rhythmic flash of light illuminating his blood.

"What about that person taking photos?"

"What?"

"At the hall. Did you find anything unusual in the crime scene photos?"

Silence.

"I can look through them. If you think the murderer's a musician, I might be able to spot something you can't —"

"No."

"But —"

"Ms. Cates, you're a person of interest in this case. Whatever you think you're doing ends now." Orion stood, his voice cold, expression shuttered. "I shouldn't have said anything."

But he had.

Leila felt this acknowledgment in the same part of her that needed to find out the truth about Carlo.

She stood and faced him, the edges of her vision dulled by exhaustion and the alcohol she'd steadily consumed for hours.

Orion possessed a conviction she'd lost tonight. His life still made sense. He believed in pursuing the truth, in the value of what he did.

A mixture of envy and hunger yawned open inside her.

Leila wanted what he had.

She wanted to walk along the edge of those cliffs and taste that strength, harden herself against her surroundings, and find renewed purpose again, no matter how temporary.

Before she could think about it, she pressed against him, felt his shoulders stiffen beneath her fingers, and lifted her face to his.

His mouth was warm and he tasted like coffee and spearmint gum. He smelled of a New York winter, warmth and cold combined, the pure metallic spark of an impending storm.

That coiled energy she felt in him snapped around her and for one heartbeat, she felt his chest hitch, his body respond.

He placed his hands on her hips and she leaned in, seeking more of his heat, his ferocious intensity.

The pressure of his hands increased and it took a few seconds for realization to penetrate the hazy fog of her mind.

He was pushing her away.

Leila stepped back, fingers touching her mouth, heated mortification rushing through her.

What the hell was she doing? He was a cop investigating her for the murder of her boyfriend and she'd fucking thrown herself at him.

"Sorry, I just…sorry," she mumbled.

He turned aside. "My guys will be at Carlo's studio by now."

She nodded, mute.

"Get some rest," he said and left.

Leila retreated to the piano, hands trembling at the life spinning out of their control.

She pushed the metronome, the precise tick reminding her of measures and boundaries.

Now that Orion was gone, the frantic *presto* pulse no longer seemed right.

She adjusted the speed, reducing it to an ominous *adagio* that boomed like thunder in her chest.

SEVEN

Leila paused at the Ansonia's main door and peered through the glass. Soft sconce lighting, nestled along the building's exterior, dimly illuminated the narrow corridor.

"A few people were loitering around earlier today, Ms. Cates," the evening doorman said discreetly. "But they left several hours ago."

"Thank you."

He opened the door and she quickly crossed the building's private entrance, stepping out through the main gates on to Broadway.

Bitter night blanketed the city, wrapping Leila in the comforting shield of darkness. Instead of catching a cab, she decided to walk.

The frigid air eased the dull throbbing along her jaw. Careful application of concealer hid most of the discoloration, but the swelling remained.

Despite finishing off a bottle of wine and sleeping for twelve hours after Orion left, the odor of embarrassment and humiliation lingered, clinging to Leila's skin.

Fractured images had filled her sleep, snapshots of piano keys scattered across a stage, bloodied naked women writhing in ecstasy, and Carlo, smiling, calling her "*Bellissima*," while icy fingers gripped her hips and pushed her away.

Leila pulled her coat tight around her and wove through the dense throngs of pedestrians crowding the sidewalk.

Her appointment would probably be useless, but the possibility it might not be had driven her out of the apartment.

That same promise fueled the masses shifting around her.

Potential was a dangerous, intoxicating drug, luring people here from all over the world by offering the greatest high of all: the possibility of more.

More money, more fame, more power, a prettier wife, a more successful husband, smarter kids, a better life packaged and offered on a plate of narcissistic greed.

The city fed off that hunger, off the frenzied energy of ambition and ego pulsing like an undercurrent through high-rises and stores, through tenements and offices, bars, classrooms, and clubs.

A well-dressed man in his early fifties exited the corner cafe and approached her.

"Excuse me, Ms. Cates?"

"Yes?"

Something about him felt vaguely familiar and she strained to remember where they'd met. Probably at one of her parents' events.

His shoulders were hunched up in a perpetual shrug and he smelled of cappuccinos and a cologne that reminded her of old men in musty rooms.

Beneath a long, black coat, he wore a conservative three-piece suit, pairing it with a red polka-dotted tie in a painfully obvious attempt to appear more whimsical than he really was.

Thinning grey hair was fastidiously combed back above his ears and the streetlights glanced off the shiny bald patch at the top of his head.

"My name is Peter Foerstner and I'm with the *New York Post-Gazette* —"

Leila walked away, her stride measured and unhurried even as her pulse quickened.

"Terrible news what happened to Carlo Belandini." He kept up with her, the smooth edges of his voice conveying a tasteful dismay. "You have my deepest sympathies."

Leila crossed 73rd, swerved through moving traffic, narrowly missed being hit by an over-enthusiastic taxi.

"Ms. Cates, all I need is a few moments of your time to talk about it.

Maybe we could have coffee?"

If it had been any other day, Leila would've been thrilled to do just that.

Peter Foerstner's tenacity, incisive prose, and almost encyclopedic knowledge of classical music made him the foremost music critic in the country.

He was also a pianist who'd once dreamed of a virtuoso career but lacked the talent to perform the very works he so deeply loved.

Under different circumstances, a conversation with him would've been every up-and-coming artist and scheming publicist's wet dream.

"I'm sorry," she murmured. "I have no comment."

"You've been gaining such momentum. It'd be a shame if this cut that short."

She stopped.

Peter drew up beside her and the crowds veered around them in an irritated surge. He stared at her swollen jaw with fascination and distaste as if she were a car wreck on the side of the highway.

"I could write an article about the life of Carlo Belandini." He adjusted and smoothed his tie. "One in which the artistic world mourns the tragic death of a gifted artist cut short in his prime. And of course the grief of his partner in life and music, a rising, young pianist on the cusp of achieving international success."

"Or?"

"Or I could write an article about his death. About how you discovered the body after a very public disagreement during what was to become Belandini's final rehearsal."

Peter picked an imaginary piece of lint off his coat sleeve with thick, blunt fingers.

"I could write about how you spent a few hours at the station and left with our city's greediest attorney, Brian Kensington, and your parents' influence over all of it." He paused. "I wonder how Columbia would feel about that, especially with the Cates Performing Arts Hall opening soon."

Leila wondered how many members of the New York Philharmonic had talked, portioning up the juicy events of that last rehearsal like choice morsels, basking in the self-importance of sharing lurid gossip.

Her smile felt brittle. "Whatever happened to journalistic integrity?"

"You've been in the arts long enough to know it's always about selling cheap melodrama, Ms. Cates." Peter touched his tie again. "You can, of course, have your say in what article I write."

Marlene.

Peter Foerstner reminded her of SMI's reigning head, his critical eyes coldly assessing how much value she could add toward his purpose.

For Peter and Marlene, artists without a high sales tag were like non-designer clothes. Without brand recognition, they were meaningless.

Musicians, eager for confirmation of their worth and acknowledgment of their potential, perpetually lay prostrate before them, grateful for whatever tiny attention was thrown their way.

Those damn photos once again flashed before Leila - *Marlene, sprawled across Carlo's bed* - and the same wildness she felt in that final rehearsal rushed through her.

Finding out what happened to Carlo meant she balanced on a precarious edge, unable to leap off or pull back. It meant a darker world of swollen jaws and scarred arms, of tall detectives in her apartment at dawn.

The same tipsiness that sent her teetering toward Orion last night now pulled her away from Peter.

"Does Barry Goldman know about this ultimatum?"

He stiffened at the mention of his editor.

"My father golfed with him two weeks ago before they went out for dinner with Daniel Shaw."

The Shaws, long-time owners of the paper, also had a long history with the Cates, ever since the families first settled in Westchester County almost a century ago.

"I don't know if Daniel would like hearing about this, either."

Peter looked away, his sausage fingers stroking that ugly tie over and over, then turned back to her.

"I think I'll take my chances," he said.

"So will I."

Leila smiled and left him on the corner, his bald head and red tie quickly swallowed up by the sea of voracious people rushing toward their next fix.

Fifteen minutes later, Leila neared the entrance to the Columbus Circle station, the smell of Peter Foerstner's cologne still stinging her nose, that cold wildness lodged in her chest.

Sayaka was already there, leaning against a metal pillar beside the escalator and texting on her phone. Her cello's hard case rested on the ground beside her.

She glanced up at Leila's approach and hurried forward.

"What happened?" She gestured at her jaw. "Are you all right?"

"Tooth emergency. Had an extraction this morning."

"Well, it's not that bad. The audience won't see it when you're onstage."

Leila wondered how many other lies her friend had told over the years.

"God, Leila." Sayaka wrapped her in a hug. "I'm so, so sorry about what happened with Carlo."

"Yeah."

Sayaka's arms pressed hard against Leila's bruised shoulders and back. The ache and smell of her friend's shampoo reminded her of Carlo's comforter.

Sayaka pulled back. "I heard the funeral is at Lake Cuomo on Sunday."

"Oh."

"Have you read the papers?"

Leila shook her head.

"Don't," Sayaka said sharply. "Assholes sensationalized all of it."

"I haven't checked my messages yet. Carlo's parents probably called about it."

"I'm assuming you'll go after the concert?" Sayaka shoved her hands in her pocket, and lightly bounced to keep warm. "You could go back and forth to Italy over the weekend, right? 'Cause you have your parents' thing next week."

"I guess."

Sayaka frowned and Leila realized how odd it must seem that her murdered boyfriend's funeral wasn't more of a priority.

She didn't want to explain anything to her. But there were things that needed to get done.

"Of course I'm going." Leila shuffled her feet. "Just haven't had a chance to plan things yet."

She squeezed Leila's bruised arm. "I can help."

"Sure. Fine." Leila pulled away. "Come on. Let's get this over with."

Sayaka kept up a steady chatter as they headed west on 59th then down Tenth Avenue.

"So I look through this suite and it's trying so hard to be experimental, when really it's just a riff off Rihm with elements of Stockhausen, except gimmicky, you know?" She gave an exasperated sigh. "And don't ask me how the hell he managed to get my email address."

Leila gave a perfunctory nod, stopping before a grimy, low-rise building, tucked between a deli and laundromat.

"You sure about this?" Sayaka asked. "Hector's not exactly the most likable person to be around. And I don't know how much you can trust—"

"I'm sure."

Trust was no longer a considering factor. If it were, Leila wouldn't have asked for Sayaka's help.

What she needed now were answers.

Sayaka looked unconvinced but pressed the button for apartment 3B. Piercing static crackled over the speaker and Leila winced.

"It's me," Sayaka said loudly.

The door buzzed open. Leila followed Sayaka up a dark stairwell, the scent of mildew and ash drifting around them.

A corpulent man stood in an open doorway on the third floor, a cigarette dangling from his fingers.

Hector Valdez, a freelance violinist who'd graduated a few years ahead of Sayaka and Leila, hovered on the outskirts of the musical community.

No one quite understood his story, especially since he told a different version to everyone he met.

Some said he grew up in the household of Diego Valente, the head of a Latin American crime family. Others said he was the illegitimate child of a famous musician and a woman from a small village.

Sayaka told Leila she'd heard he was an orphan from San Jose, a child prodigy who'd fought his way out of Costa Rica to Brazil, Russia, and Germany before finally arriving in the US.

Leila heard Hector play years ago, a forgettable event in which he sight-read the music, promptly picked up his check once the applause stopped, and negotiated a separate concert with the presenter at twice the price.

Hector was the ultimate gigger, faking his way through every performance, networking and wheedling deals, shrugging off the criticisms of the Marlenes and Peters by investing so little of himself that his very shallowness protected him from failure.

He ruled the freelance community like a godfather, doling out paying work to desperate musicians who couldn't make their rent, rewarding allegiance and loyalty above all else.

He nodded at Sayaka before looking at Leila. A prominent forehead and nose overshadowed his face and his coarse skin glistened with a layer of sweat.

"Leila Cates."

She nodded.

"Come in."

They followed him into a boiling hot apartment that smelled of unwashed linens and cat piss.

"Have a seat. Sorry it's not much." He gave an exaggerated shrug that jiggled his jowls. "What can I say? I'm just a lowly musician."

"We all are," Sayaka said, eyeing a dusty chair with distaste. "And you make more money than us."

"Please," Hector scoffed, yet didn't deny it.

He settled on a lumpy futon, took a swig of Coke, and tapped the end of his cigarette on an overflowing ashtray.

Sayaka opted for the clean corner of a folding chair and Leila took a seat near a large corner desk.

EMMA RAVELING

"Quite the honor to have you here." Dark, shrewd eyes shone through a haze of smoke. "Terrible thing what happened to Carlo. Sorry to hear it."

"Thanks." Leila gave the standard greeting expected in their world. "I heard you're busy. Playing a lot."

"Yeah, yeah." He took a long drag and exhaled. "Playing in Argentina next month."

He waited expectantly for a response.

"Really?" Leila tried to sound impressed. "Where?"

"Mendoza Music Festival."

"Doesn't Alfredo Bogoya run that now?" Leila vaguely remembered Joshua introducing her to a small, nervous man at an event several months ago.

Hector nodded, a pleased look in his eyes. "He's a friend," he said with false modesty. "After the last director left, I made the necessary introductions for him to get the position."

He leaned back on the futon, stretching his arms across the back. The buttons on his shirt strained against his bulging stomach, making him seem wider.

Two cats slinked along the doorway leading to the rest of the apartment, glittering eyes watching the visitors with calculated caution.

"You know, Alfredo's always looking for pianists for the festival," he said speculatively. "I can probably get you in, hook you up with some other musicians."

Sayaka shifted, looking slightly embarrassed.

Leila raised her brow. "I only play chamber music with people I choose."

"Of course, of course." He readjusted his approach. "Guess you must be busy with all your solo concerts."

Leila remained silent.

"I don't know if I could get you in anyway." He put out his cigarette. "I've been so busy." He waved his hand. "You know how it is. One concert after the other, traveling, on the phone."

"Yeah."

"Of course, I'm here to help out my fellow musicians whenever I can. We all have to stick together in this business, right?"

"Sure."

Hector leaned forward, dark eyes boring into her, trying to see all her secrets.

"What can I do for you, Leila?"

"Heard you have other talents besides music."

"Maybe. People exaggerate sometimes."

"Can you access restricted files on a protected site?"

"Depends on the site."

"The NYPD database."

Sayaka straightened. "What?"

Hector's mouth curved into a sly smile. "You want to see what the cops know about Carlo."

His extra-musical skills had added a significant chunk to his income over the years. Dozens of students owed their graduation to Hector's handiwork with the school server.

"Leila, I don't know if —"

"How much?" Leila's eyes locked on to Hector.

"It's your first time." He shrugged. "No charge."

But she'd owe him and he never forgot a favor.

She nodded.

Hector hefted his large frame off the futon with a grunt and settled at his desk. While his hands flew over the keyboard with surprising dexterity, Sayaka slid into the seat beside her.

"What are you doing?" she whispered.

Leila kept her eyes on Hector's monitor. "Finding out what the cops have so far."

"Why?"

Leila looked at her. "Because I want to know the truth."

Sayaka blinked a few times, then turned away.

For the next minute, Hector's heavy breathing and the rapid clicking of his keyboard were the only sounds in the apartment.

"There we go," he murmured.

A log-in page featuring the NYPD logo splashed across the monitor.

"Can you get in?" Leila pressed.

"Hang on."

A few more clicks.

The screen changed and a file directory popped up.

Hector chuckled and finished off his soda. His curly, black hair glistened under the harsh light of a halogen lamp. "What do you need?"

Leila leaned in and scanned the listed files.

She pointed to a folder. "Crime scene photos."

Hector double-clicked on it, opening a window with several dozen image files.

"I want to see all of them."

They flashed across the screen in rapid succession, snapshots of what haunted her memories and dreams.

Sayaka's harsh intake of breath, Hector's mumblings, and the reek of cat piss faded, leaving behind only the stark crimson of Carlo's death.

"Wait."

Hector paused.

"Go back two photos."

He clicked back, bringing up a close-up of Carlo's hand.

The beautiful fingers that had danced across her skin and brought music to life with a gesture lay palm side up in a pool of blood.

Between his thumb and index finger, a distinct pattern in blue ink was smudged against his skin.

Sayaka leaned in. "What is that?"

"Looks like a letter." Hector clicked the mouse and the image flipped over. "It's inverted."

It was the letter R.

The way it smeared across Carlo's palm meant it transferred off something he'd been holding.

"I've seen that before," Leila murmured.

The R was distinct, a signature of some sort. The bottom corner of the letter swirled up with a grand flourish.

Sayaka rested her hands on the back of Hector's chair. "I feel like I've seen it, too."

Leila remembered Carlo's clean, manicured hands at rehearsal. The mark hadn't been there earlier in the day.

"Is there any way you could get this to me —"

"Already done."

Hector transferred all the case files to a flash drive, ejected it, and handed it over.

"Thanks." She headed for the door.

"Anything for a friend," he said.

And someday he'd come calling, asking her to return the favor.

Sayaka caught up with her on Tenth Avenue as she waited for a cab.

"Leila!" She pulled up beside her, breathing hard, cello case strapped to her back. "Why did you leave?"

"Sorry. I have stuff to do."

"You didn't even wait for me!"

Leila raised her hand, impatient. "I thought you were going to hang out with Hector."

Sayaka ran her fingers through her hair. "First you blow up in rehearsal, then you're running around the streets at night. Now you're doing illegal shit with the cops and —"

"And what?"

"It's not like you."

Sayaka was far back on Leila's list of things to address, behind Carlo's murderer, the cops, the concert, her parents, Joshua, Marlene, even Peter Foerstner.

"I know I've seen that R somewhere," she said flatly. "I want to go home and check."

"Then let me come with you. Maybe I can help."

Leila didn't have the energy to argue. "Fine."

An awkward silence fell between the two women during the cab ride back. Sayaka glanced at Leila several times, but said nothing, letting the obnoxious commentary from talk radio fill the space instead.

"Ms. Cates." The doorman called out as they crossed the lobby. "A delivery arrived for you."

He pulled a package from the storage room and carried it into the elevator for her.

The plainly wrapped box came up to Leila's hip and listed the Booth Hill Institute in Tarrytown, New York as the return address.

It had been sent to her, not her parents.

"Were you expecting something?" Sayaka asked.

Leila shook her head, her hands cold and chest tight.

She dragged the box into her apartment, desperation intensifying with each second, needing to open it in the same way she needed Hector to pry open those sealed folders.

"You think your Mom sent it?"

Leila grabbed a pair of scissors and attacked the tape. "No."

The box fell away, revealing its contents.

Later, Leila would wish she'd waited, tempered that desperate curiosity for a few more minutes until she regained control and found her balance.

The music stand was the same model used by the New York Philharmonic, the same stand that crushed Carlo's skull and brain into pieces.

A five by seven black-and-white photo was taped to it.

The frozen faces of Paul and Helen Cates greeted her. Beside them, Marlene Soltano gave a distracted partial smile, her eyes focused on something to the left of the camera.

An impressive array of artists lined up beside her: Heinrich Descher, Anastasia Rossen, Elliot Frank, and her teacher, Vladimir Markov.

Leila stood in front of them all, carrying a bouquet of roses, her face beaming with triumph.

It was the night she'd won the Juilliard Concerto Competition. Taking the top prize at the conservatory had immediately brought her to the attention of Marlene and several other major concert presenters and artists, ultimately paving the way for her win at the New York International Music

Competition.

That night was the start of everything leading to her Lincoln Center debut and the discovery of Carlo's broken skull.

Leila had never seen it before.

Two items framed the photo. A pair of black lace panties hung off the left corner of the stand.

Leila recognized them as hers. She thought she'd misplaced it a few months ago.

On the right corner hung a light pink thong, the delicate straps and sheer material designed specifically for seduction and flirtation, not practicality.

Leila didn't recognize it.

Sayaka did. "That's mine."

Leila stared at the frozen faces trapped in the photograph.

"Why is it there?" Sayaka's voice tapped a brisk staccato against the parquet floor. "Who sent this —"

"The killer put it there."

"What?" Sayaka's voice grew shrill. "What do you mean—"

"Carlo's killer wants to tell me what happened between you two." Leila turned to her friend. "I already knew, though. Did you forget it at his studio?"

Sayaka paled, her mouth parting into a small "O".

"Carlo had a photo of you there. Along with a bunch of others."

A sheen of moisture glistened across her eyes. "Leila, I —"

"Get out."

"Please. Let me explain —"

"Get out!"

The deafening silence that followed was the roar of frustration and rage, the howling awareness that there would never be a time when Leila could forget her friend had done this, that she alone would suffer the consequences of Carlo's actions while he lay buried six feet under, his life celebrated and mourned.

The silence screamed.

It screamed through Leila's lungs, screamed through her stomach and chest, across the paintings and furnishings entombed in this cold, cold mausoleum, screamed into Sayaka until she grabbed her cello and fled into the night.

EIGHT

"Ma'am?"

An earnest looking cop stepped in front of Leila, his short hair still damp from a shower. He didn't look old enough to drink.

"Are you all right?"

Officers in puffy jackets milled about the entry hall, navy blue uniforms like additional dabs of paint in front the Rothko.

A burly cop sneezed, his face flushed with fever. He noisily blew his nose and tossed the damp tissue into a large standing vase on the floor.

With one gesture, he'd transformed a piece of art worth nearly a million dollars into a trash can.

"Yes." Leila wrapped her arms around her stomach. "I'm fine."

"Better not be contaminating my crime scene, O'Malley." Orion entered the apartment and gave the sick cop a freezing look. "Or you'll be writing up parking tickets for the next year."

O'Malley scowled but removed the used kleenex from the vase.

"Maybe you should go into another room." The young officer glanced at her swollen jaw.

"This is my apartment."

"I understand, but I think it's in your best interest—"

"I got it." Orion's long stride quickly consumed the distance between them. "Thanks."

The officer gave a smart nod and left.

Orion stopped before her, the cold clinging to his coat and matching the distance in his eyes.

Snap. Snap. A camera's rhythmic flash clicked behind him, the lights bouncing off tonight's star.

A crime scene investigator removed the black and white photo from the music stand. Next were both pairs of underwear, his gloved hands carefully placing them in clear evidence bags.

Leila thought embarrassment over her drunken neediness would make it difficult to face Orion.

But as blank-faced strangers examined her panties and Sayaka's thong, she realized embarrassment, like trust, had set sail a long time ago.

"Here to comfort me?" she said.

"I'm taking your statement."

"I already gave one. Where's Detective Brogan?"

Without his partner's balancing presence, Orion seemed restless, untethered among the sea of other officers.

"Following up on something else."

"On what?"

Orion glanced at the apartment entrance. The doorman stood just outside, speaking to an officer with agitated movements. A few neighbors gathered around him, craning their necks to peer inside.

"We can do this here or at the station," he said flatly.

Leila waited another moment, then led the way to the music room.

Orion closed the door, cocooning them in dark silence. Leila turned on the standing lamp near the piano and a soft, pale light cast a triangular glow.

He leaned against the wall beside the sofa, his face concealed in the matte darkness outside the light's path.

A memory flashed before Leila, of him standing in these whispery shadows with the fragile light of dawn rising behind him, and her leaning forward, needing something she couldn't articulate.

She poured herself a glass of brandy at the room's corner bar and settled at the piano, seeking the familiar comfort of the keys.

"Who took your statement?"

"I don't remember his name. Short, bald, kind of a long nose —"

"Shit. Davidson," Orion muttered.

"Not good?"

"He's a rat scuttling for a big win before he gets his pension. Did he ask about your face?"

"Yeah and he asked where I was last night and today."

"What'd you say?"

"I was home alone, trying to sleep off a really bad toothache. Then I went to the dentist this morning to get it extracted."

The lies had come easily, slipping from her lips cool and crisp, and she'd wondered if it was the same for everyone, if Carlo, Sayaka, Marlene and all the others lied with the same ease with which they breathed.

He digested that. "You got someone who can back that up?"

"Yes." Reality could always be shaped by Cates money.

Orion crossed his arms and Leila wondered if she'd passed his test.

"You said this is your parents' place but I haven't seen them.'"

"They've been in Idaho for the past month." She took a few sips, savoring the fire racing down her throat. "They're arriving tomorrow."

Orion shifted, pulled out a small notepad and pen from his coat pocket. "Was anyone else here with you?"

"No."

"Are you lying?"

"No."

"Then why did your doorman say you came home with your friend, the girl who," he flipped back a page in his notebook, "carries a big instrument strapped to her back?"

Leila turned the glass in her hands, her fingertips tracing the intricate scrolling design etched into it. "I didn't want to get her involved."

"You mean Sayaka."

"Yes."

The acknowledgment lay bitter on her tongue.

Until that moment, she'd been unable to say it aloud, unable to tell that Davidson cop, his large nose sniffing out his legacy, about the pink, delicate thong dangling on the stand.

Saying it aloud took those hidden photos out of Carlo's studio, out of this apartment, and thrust them into the camera's flash and the unrelenting spotlight of centerstage.

"One of the panties belonged to her. I —" She cleared her throat. "I told her I knew about her and Carlo. She left before I called the police."

"Where were you before you came back together?"

Leila didn't answer.

"I told you to stay out of it," he said.

"I can't do that."

"I can arrest you for interfering."

"If you planned on doing that, you would've done it already."

"I placed my fucking neck on the line and if Davidson finds out —"

"He won't. Anything new in the investigation?"

The shadows around his tall form shifted restlessly. "You said it wasn't about bringing Carlo back."

"It's not."

"So what's it about?"

"You told me what you see when you look at me," she said slowly. "Someone who had it easy. Someone who killed her boyfriend because he stepped out of line."

Orion remained silent.

"Do you know what I see?" She looked at him. "A life that wasn't real. I want to know what's real."

Silence drifted between them, an odd pitch both dissonant and harmonious.

"All right," he finally said.

Leila put her drink down.

"It ain't pretty."

She waited.

He exhaled. "I talked to Marlene today. Alexis, too, and several of the others."

The other women. "And?"

"And Marlene slept with Carlo off and on. Whenever she got a little lonely." He rubbed his jaw. "With the exception of Alexis, most only spent one night with him."

There was no sympathy in Orion's voice, nothing indicating cheap consolation.

"Obviously, there are others we still need to speak to."

Leila wondered if Sayaka would look at him with the same pale fear with which she'd faced her.

"What about the ones who went in and out of the hall earlier that night?"

"We've checked out dozens of people and everyone has an alibi for the time of his death." He paused. "But we can't verify Marlene and Alexis' whereabouts. Marlene says she was alone at the office, working late."

"And Alexis?"

I loved him.

Leila gripped the edge of the piano bench hard.

"Says she was home alone," Orion said.

"You believe her?"

"Shouldn't I?"

"She hates me. She wanted Carlo for herself."

Orion shook his head. "She wouldn't kill the man she wanted."

"But you said this was a crime of rage. She could've snapped, made a mistake —"

"And you said a musician wouldn't make a mistake like that."

Orion turned to her, his head entering the triangle patch of light, the lamp's glow making the edges of his face blurred and fuzzy like a soft-focus lens.

"First impressions are rarely accurate. Sometimes we have to change our initial assumptions."

Leila stared at him. "You don't think it was done out of rage?"

"No, the rage was there. Takes a large amount of force to push that stand through someone's skull." He moved back, out of the light. "But I thought this happened because of Carlo. Because of his flaws, actions. Maybe he pissed the wrong person off, owed a little too much money, slept with someone's wife."

"And now?"

"Now I think this has something to do with you," he said quietly.

Leila thought of that black and white photo, the smiles trapped beneath the glossy surface, and a shiver raced down her spine.

"Why?"

"To frame you for his murder." He gestured to the door. "Whoever's doing this is toying with you by sending this stuff over. Since your parents are such public figures, it'd be easy to assume it was about them, but the package was —"

"Addressed to me."

The fury directed at Carlo had really been directed at her. This wasn't just about making her responsible for his death.

It was about making her responsible for that murderous rage.

Had Carlo known his killer? Had he fought back or stood there, his mouth partially open, as surprised as Sayaka, beneath the fatal blow?

No report from the coroner's office was listed in the file directory Hector accessed. But that didn't mean nothing had been found.

"Did the coroner say anything? About anything unusual on Carlo?"

Orion stilled. "She hasn't filed a report yet."

"I know," Leila said hastily. "Just thought she might've shared something with you or your partner."

A long silence.

"How do you know she hasn't filed a report yet?" He tapped the tip of his pen against the notepad. "What did you—"

The sound of a commotion echoed through the closed door.

"Get your fucking hands off me if you don't want a lawsuit your great-grandkids will be paying off," a cold voice barked.

The door swung open and Brian Kensington strode in, eyes spitting fury.

"Detective, you better have one hell of a fucking reason to be alone with my client right now."

Orion flipped a page in his notepad and jotted something down before replying. "Ms. Cates and I were just talking."

"Talking," Brian repeated.

"Don't think there's any crime against —"

"Detective Frazier." Brian's face narrowed, his palpable anger wringing the air out of the room. "You get my client alone, shut the door, and question her without her lawyer, a warrant, or anyone else's presence and you think I'm going to let it go?"

Orion continued scribbling in his notepad.

"Who do you think you are?" Brian said.

Orion closed the notepad and returned it to his coat pocket.

Brian advanced toward him, his lean frame tightening and pulling in on itself.

"I don't care how many cases you closed or whose ass you had to fucking kiss to get your promotion. You think attaching detective in front of your name protects you?"

Orion tilted his chin, hands shoved in his pocket as if to keep from punching him, and looked down at Brian with glacial eyes.

"You ever talk to my client without my presence again," Brian took another step, his nose inches from Orion's neck, the top of his head almost bumping against his nose, "you'll be back at your old neighborhood, riding the back of a garbage truck and hammering construction like the rest of your buddies. I will screw you so hard you won't be able to tell which way is up."

Orion smiled. "That's what your wife said."

"Fuck you. Get out."

"Ms. Cates." Orion nodded at her and pulled away from the wall.

He stopped beside the coffee table, his gaze caught on the bright centerpiece she'd placed the towel-wrapped ice in last night.

Orion picked up the bowl and looked inside, running his hand over the smooth ceramic surface as if wondering where it went.

"Pretty," he murmured.

"Yeah," she said, surprised.

"Where's it from?"

"Stockholm."

Brian edged closer to the table. "Leave."

Orion placed the bowl back on the table and calmly walked out.

Brian erupted in a scathing torrent of words, a blistering rant on the dangers of not using her fucking brains and letting a poser cop manipulate her.

But Leila didn't hear any of it.

All she saw was the tiny piece of folded paper now resting at the bottom of that bowl.

****

The screen told its own story.

The following morning, during the hushed stillness of dawn, Leila settled at her desk and combed through the files on the flash drive.

Next to her laptop, the centerpiece bowl that had once graced the music room now brightened the desk, its vivid colors a clashing counterpoint to the darkness flashing across the screen.

Leila had moved the bowl late last night and she now rubbed the smooth ceramic edge back and forth as she studied a photo, the action calming something inside her.

The close-up of Carlo's pale face revealed a serene expression, devoid of pain or fear or shock. With his closed eyes and slack mouth, he looked asleep.

Leila wondered if Orion felt this jarring dissonance on the job everyday. Understanding someone's death meant unearthing the entirety of that person's life, the accolades and beautiful homages lining up beside the porn pics stashed on the computer, the twisted roots buried away from the glaring light of day.

A tenuous line separated one person's desire to live and the intent of another to end it, and in their initial notes from the crime scene, Ian and

Orion had presented a narrative for either side.

Ian - with his kind smile and parental weariness - believed she was the killer. He was the one who'd brought her in for further questioning.

Orion's succinct report didn't clear her of suspicion. But he'd noted Leila lacked the physical strength to carry out the crime.

Professional music stands were sturdy, their heaviness designed for long-term durability.

Lifting and swinging one with sufficient force to crack Carlo's skull required the kind of strength that had also pinned her against the wall and dragged her across his studio.

Marlene was in her late forties, but maintained a body of someone half her age. Her thin, toned physique came from a rigid regimen of obsessive clean eating and endless hours of pilates, yoga, and workouts with her trainer.

Alexa didn't have the same privileges as Marlene, but she was a strong, healthy twenty-seven-year-old. Nearly six feet tall, she had large, capable hands that made her violin seem small.

Leila clicked the photo, closed the laptop, and looked out the window.

The snowfall threatening to emerge over the past few days now swallowed the city, the hard, fast flurries transforming the sky into a fog of grey.

Sayaka was also tall.

An avid runner with a lean, muscular build, she possessed a strong frame built from years of carrying her cello.

Leila stretched, the knotted muscles in her shoulders and neck creaking in protest, and headed to the music room. She picked up the folded paper resting on the piano and re-read the words that hummed in her ears from the moment the apartment emptied out the previous night.

I follow the flaws. You follow the music.

Brian had rightly advised caution. Orion could be luring Leila into his web to entrap her for Carlo's murder.

But amid an overwhelming sea of lies, the detective had somehow become her buoy of truth.

Leila's world of concert stages and building dedications was his unknown, just as his world of bruised jaws and bloody skulls was hers.

Making sense of the noise would require both of them.

Leila left her apartment. Broadway greeted her with a bitter, impersonal chill that slashed through bone and seeped into the marrow.

During the cab ride to midtown, she checked the arts section of the *New York Post-Gazette* website on her phone.

No salacious article on her or her parents, or on the life and death of the great Carlo Belandini.

Peter Foerstner had yet to wield his pen.

Her phone vibrated with a familiar number.

Leila declined the call, knowing Sayaka would leave another voice message, another quiet plea asking for an opportunity to explain.

She wasn't ready to give it to her.

Her phone buzzed again. This time, she answered.

"God, Leila, where have you been?"

Joshua's voice, reedy with irritated relief, grated against her ear.

Snow swirled, a white hush clinging to the steel edges and asphalt curves of the city. Pristine powder clung to the sidewalks and streets, concealing the ugly grime, the lurid ambition and greed pulsing beneath.

"I've been trying to reach you for two days!"

"I know."

"Then why the hell didn't you pick up? I wanted to check on you after you left the station, but Charlotte was losing her mind and I spent the entire night convincing René to take over for Carlo or we were going to lose the whole damn concert —"

"René Chauveau is conducting tomorrow?"

"Don't you check your messages? For crying out loud, Leila, you don't return anyone's calls and with everything that's been going on…" He let out a long exhale. "I was going over to your place this afternoon to make sure you were still alive."

The cab rounded the park and headed down Broadway. "I've been laying low."

A pause. "What happened last night?"

"Nothing."

"That's not what Helen said."

"When did you speak to her?"

"Paul and Helen are here at the offices right now. They haven't called you yet?"

"No." The cab stopped at the corner of Fifty-Seventh and Seventh. Leila paid and stepped out into the white fury consuming the city.

"Well, they got in just before the snow started and they've been catching Marlene up on everything," Joshua continued, his voice strained. "Meanwhile, I've been trying to handle all the press and details for the concert tomorrow and René and Marlene have been giving me shit and you've been gone and —"

"I'm here. I'll be up in a minute."

Posters for upcoming concerts lined Carnegie Hall's iconic brick and brownstone exterior. Several familiar faces and names, either from Juilliard or the SMI roster, leaped out at her.

A poster for the Berlin Philharmonic's New York stop on their North American tour hung alongside one for a new age singer she vaguely recognized.

A few television talk shows had raved about the entertainer who'd uncovered his so-called musical genius at the age of forty-two after a spiritual journey to find himself in India and Tibet. A mere two years later and he was already performing at Carnegie Hall, courtesy of Bring 'Em Love Productions.

The new age singer's poster had a large "Sold Out" banner across it.

The Berlin Philharmonic's did not.

Leila carefully crossed Fifty-Seventh, gloved hands deep in her pockets, chin tucked beneath the scarf wrapped around her neck.

She pressed the buzzer for the white building directly across from the hall. With a discreet ping, the door opened and she took the elevator to the top floor.

Marlene sat across from Paul and Helen Cates on the leather couch in the main reception area. They were deep in conversation, the air thick with smug righteousness and unwavering faith.

"This was not what we agreed to."

Helen Cates spoke hard and fast, her words knifing through the thick wall of insulation shielding her from the truths of her life.

"Do you know what it's been like?" Marlene sipped her wine. "The press have been calling non-stop and now Peter Foerstner is threatening to do some sort of expose on —"

"Leila didn't cause any of this and she deserves that concert tomorrow. After everything we've done—"

"She gets the concert, Helen," Marlene said wearily. "I just don't know what'll happen once it's over."

"Hello," Leila said.

Helen jerked. Dark curls were loosely pulled back, a few tendrils framing a strongly defined face: straight brows, tall nose, sharp jawline. A beige cashmere scarf draped her broad shoulders, softening the edges of her tall, square frame.

"What happened to your face?"

Leila removed her coat. "I went to the dentist."

"Christopher? He didn't tell me —"

"I went to someone else."

"Marlene, did you know about —"

"No." Marlene stared at Leila's jaw as if it were a blemish she could carve out. "I don't think it'll be visible onstage."

The sharp planes of Paul Cates' handsome face had mellowed over the past few years, gaining a certain sameness, a uniform blandness that all men his age and in his societal circle seemed to have.

Paul gave her a wobbly, distracted smile. "Honey."

"Hi, Dad."

His phone pinged and his attention vanished.

"Brian told us what happened last night." Helen shook her head. "All you had to do was stay out of it."

"That package was sent to me. I had to call the police."

"Did you also have to be alone with that detective?"

Leila moved toward the sofa without replying.

Marlene slid over to make room and winced. The beige edge of a bandage peeked out from beneath her pant leg.

"Are you okay?"

"Pushed too hard during a session with Pierre. It's nothing. Just a twisted ankle."

Leila settled beside her, something cold slithering through her belly. "When did you hurt it?"

"Yesterday." Marlene's flat, hard eyes studied her, probing for any hint of weakness. "Are you sure you can play tomorrow? Simone Harrison can step in. She has the Brahms in her fingers."

The concert's draw was no longer just the gruesome specter of Carlo's death; it was also about witnessing Leila's survival.

People wanted to see her triumph over grief and become the bloodied gladiator standing alone in the arena. The stage demanded a moving display of grit and tenacity, a story about an inspiring comeback despite tragic suffering.

Leila was now the headliner in a performance selling the American Dream.

The only way to extinguish the sordidness of murder was with a spectacular performance that would be remembered for the ages, a concert that would become an immortal part of her legacy.

"I can do it."

Leila wondered if Marlene ever thought of her while her Pilates-toned legs were wrapped around Carlo's hips.

"Of course she can do it." Helen slid over a glass of chardonnay. "But she doesn't need those press vultures harassing her. Have a drink, Leila. You're wound up so tight your shoulders are up to your ears."

"I don't need —"

"You need to focus on what's important."

"You do seem a little pale." Marlene's gaze once again locked on to her jaw. "You're sure about this?"

Leila drank, her mind swirling like the snow, winding around Marlene with her flat, hard eyes and twisted ankle, maybe her shin bruised from a kick.

She drained the glass and said, "I told you, I'm fine."

"She'll be fine," Helen affirmed.

"'Course she will," Paul added jovially. "She's a Cates. Right, honey?"

"Dress rehearsal will be at the hall three hours before the concert," Marlene said slowly, still examining, evaluating. "René wants to run through the concerto with you."

Leila nodded. "Where's Joshua?"

Marlene gestured at a closed door. With a politely murmured excuse, Leila escaped.

She knocked and nudged the door open. "Hi."

Joshua waved her in, phone caught between his ear and shoulder.

"Yes." He swiveled his chair and faced the small window behind his desk. "I understand, Lars, but is there anything we can do?"

A long pause.

Leila rarely entered Josh's private office. Most of their meetings had taken place in SMI's main reception area or backstage.

"If you think his fee is too high, we can re-negotiate." Joshua swiveled back and shook his head. *Hang on*, he mouthed.

On his desk, delicate crystal figurines of a cello, conductor's baton, and piano sparkled beside an elegant Waterford vase and a pile of scores.

"You're bringing Vassily and Forman." Joshua frowned at his computer monitor, clicked the mouse. "The festival should have enough budget to bring Alex."

The music were all for solo piano, probably a new batch of manuscripts sent in by desperate composers.

Leila sifted through the sheets, hearing the opening melodic statement, the rhythmic articulation and harmonic coloring in her mind, and rejecting them all within a few measures.

Nothing to say. Lacks originality. No voice. Weak construction.

About a quarter of the way through the pile, she stopped.

"That man is determined to run the festival into the ground." Joshua put down the phone and noticed her expression. "What?"

"Who sent these?"

"I gave that stack of new music to you months ago," he said, irritated. "Those are my copies. I don't know why I bother when you won't even make the effort to look through them."

Displayed across the top in a large, bold font was the title along with the dedication beneath it.

Fantasiestucke for Solo Piano, Op. 10, No.1
for Leila Cates

The composer was R. Wynford.

A signature was scribbled above the name. The artistic scrawl in royal blue ink sharply contrasted with the printed black notes, standing out in a way that made you notice.

Made you remember.

The slanted R elegantly curved at the end, the bottom corner swirling up with a distinct, grand flourish.

NINE

The morning of her concert, Leila stood in a familiar place.

She knocked on the closed door tucked between an ensemble rehearsal space and an ear-training classroom, the muted sounds of horns, winds, and strings drifting around her.

"Come in."

Vladimir sat at one of the two Steinway grands in his studio, fingers resting on the keys, his face slightly flushed in a way that meant he'd either been making music or drinking, usually both.

"Leila." He stood, gave her a hearty embrace and a kiss on both cheeks. His large hands clasped her shoulders, sure and strong, and he peered at her face with the same curious concern he examined a score. "What happened to your face?"

"Dentist."

"They're all con artists. How are you?"

"Surviving."

"Smart girl." Vladimir released his grip, opened the small refrigerator beside his desk, took out a small carton of orange juice. "That is all we can do."

He pulled out a plastic cup and Thermos he kept in the bottom drawer of his desk. After pouring out a cup of juice, he splashed in a generous amount of vodka.

Leila accepted the drink and settled in a chair by the window overlooking Sixty-fourth street.

She nodded at the open score on the piano stand. "Are you performing Tchaikovsky?"

"In Prague next month," he said modestly, joining her at the window.

Vladimir studied her over the rim of his cup. "What happened was terrible," he said roughly. "Terrible."

"I took some time to be alone."

"Good."

"But I'm still playing tonight."

He waved his hand. "Of course you are."

Leila paused, the dismissive gesture and carelessness of his tone catching in her chest.

Sometimes, Leila thought Vladimir didn't understand how much she looked up to him, counted on him.

Vladimir had never steered her wrong and if he told her at that moment to cancel her New York debut, she would've done so.

"Do you think I shouldn't play?"

Light peeked in and out of the overcast sky and a shadow fell, casting Vladimir's sagging, exuberant face in something cold and hard and brittle.

"You are ready," was all he said.

Leila crossed her legs, pushed aside her disappointment. "Came across a photo of us after I won the school concerto competition a few years ago. Remember that?"

"Of course. You played Rachmaninoff well."

Leila smiled, relieved at the acknowledgment.

Vladimir despised competitions, declaring art wasn't the same as racing horses on a track and couldn't be measured by objective criteria. Playing faster, louder, or with less missed notes meant nothing to him and he made sure everyone knew it.

His frequent, vocal objections fell on deaf ears. Judging the conservatory's annual competition was like serving jury duty.

No one liked doing it, but it was a requirement for faculty.

"It feels like it was just yesterday and now I'm playing at Lincoln

Center." Leila sipped the tart drink and brought the cup close, resting the bottom edge against her stomach. "Everything happens so fast it just blurs."

All the competitions and tours and performances jumbled together into a haze, floating across her mind in the same way the sounds and dreams of practicing students echoed down the hall.

Vladimir placed his cup on the windowsill. "Many years ago, while I was still at the conservatory, Neuhaus told our studio a story about two pianists. Both were top musicians in their school, with the potential to become great artists. One day, an impresario arrived after hearing of their great talent. He offered them a chance at a solo career, the opportunity to play in the world's greatest halls."

Vladimir shuffled his feet, his bulky frame unable to find a comfortable position on the plastic chair.

"But that offer meant they had to make a decision. It meant a life of constant travel and focus." He spread his hands. "No home, no family. Only service to the art."

Outside, the light shifted again, the subtle change in color reminding Leila of a sparkling passage in the first movement of the Ravel concerto.

She strained to imprint the pale coloring inside herself, to store the precise change in her mind so she could use it as inspiration the next time she performed the piece.

"The first pianist, a refined, elegant musician, said he was not willing to do what the impresario asked. He lived so he could play music; he did not play music to live. After he finished his studies, graduating with honors, he returned to his village and became a farmer. He continued to play the piano everyday, practicing all the great works and keeping them in his fingers while learning new repertoire. But he played for himself and created magnificent music inside of his home, his only audience being his lovely wife and two sons.

"When he died, he took all that music, that priceless gift for expressing in sound what it meant to be human, with him. No one had heard him play so no one knew the caliber of the pianist buried into the ground. But his wife and sons, those who loved him, grieved for the simple man who tilled the ground and worked with his hands until the last day of his life."

Vladimir picked up his cup and took a quick, hard drink.

"The second pianist accepted the impresario's offer," he continued. "He embarked on a big concert tour and became a sensation. His concerts moved people, touched them because they heard a truth they did not realize they knew, a truth that could only be in expressed in music. Audiences raved, held their experience with his music in their hearts and when he died, there was a grand funeral. People crossed great distances to pay their respects. Everyone knew his name and his art. But no one knew his heart."

Leila thought of Carlo, lying on stage in a pool of blood like a damn Shakespearean tragedy, the stash of photos hidden within the pages of his scores, and Peter Foerstner, stroking his ugly tie, contemplating which image to present to the world.

"Neuhaus asked us which of these two we wanted to be? The first pianist who remained pure to his art, who played solely for himself, keeping his great gift hidden so that it died with him, unheard and lost in that small grave? Or the second who lived a life alone so he could share his gift, his music remembered by those immeasurably enriched by it?"

Leila put down her cup, glanced out the window. There was only one answer.

"Music is meant to be heard. There is no worse fate for an artist than being forgotten, Leila," Vladimir said gruffly. "Remind yourself of this each time you play, every time you take the stage. It is another opportunity for you to say something that has never been said before, to give the audience something they can hold on to. Remember that tonight and you will be a success."

Ten minutes later, Vladimir's next student arrived and Leila left his studio, her hands warm and tingling with vodka, her chest feeling colder than when she arrived.

On the first floor, she wove through the tangle of students carrying instruments of all sizes, her head down so she wouldn't meet their round, curious gazes, and entered the school's administrative office.

"Leila." Adam McConnell, assistant to the Communications Director, was working behind the counter. His dour face brightened, lips stretching into a broad, toothy smile. "What a surprise."

"I came by to visit Vladimir."

"He must be so proud of you." His gaze flickered over her jaw. "I'm really looking forward to your concert tonight."

Adam glanced around, checking if his co-workers had noticed that the current hot piece of gossip was talking to him.

They did.

Satisfied, he turned to her and deliberately dropped his voice. "I just think it's so brave how you're doing this."

Leila wanted to claw the avid fascination off his face. "Thanks."

"Have they found anything?" He rested his elbows on the counter, leaned in, and Leila had an image of a wolf poised over its prey, ready to leap in for the kill. "You know, about who did it?"

"No. Nothing yet."

He pulled back, disappointed. "Don't know what the world is coming to. Something awful like that happening to a great artist like him."

"Yeah."

Adam patted her hand, the move sympathetic and pompous in equal measures. "What can I do to help?"

"I actually need you to look up someone who studied with Heinrich Descher recently. He uses the name R. Wynford for his compositions now, but I don't think he went by that while he was here."

The biography on R. Wynford's simple website stated he'd studied here with Descher. Leila searched the conservatory's alumni directory but had found no one by that name.

"I'm guessing there's a reason you need to look this person up?" Adam asked delicately.

She looked away, then back. "There's something I want to do for Carlo's funeral."

Glee flashed through his eyes at this new piece of information.

"Of course." He faced the monitor on the counter and began typing.

"You said recently?"

"Yeah. Like over the past decade, probably in the Master's program."

Descher only taught graduate-level composition.

"Well, that was easy. He's in here with the same name. Robert Wynford. This was four years ago."

The same year she won the school competition.

"He was doing his doctorate with Descher."

Nothing on Wynford's bio indicated he'd finished it. "Why wasn't he listed in the alumni directory?"

"Can't really tell you that, Leila. Confidential info. Sorry."

She leaned in, lowered her voice. "Is there anything you can do? I need to get in touch with him fast. I want to perform one of his works at the funeral."

Adam greedily swallowed that new tidbit. "Well, he's not in the directory because he left after the first year."

"Why?"

"Doesn't say." He shrugged. "People come in and out of here all the time for all sorts of reasons."

Forgotten.

Countless starry-eyed musicians, actors, and dancers who came to the city filled with potential vanished into oblivion every year.

"Looks like he filed some kind of grievance with the school before he left." Adam clicked the mouse a few times. "But I can't tell what kind because his entire file is inaccessible. System has it on lockdown."

"Is that normal?"

He turned, picked up a sheaf of papers from the inbox and removed the paperclip. "Depends on what kind of grievance was filed. If it was something that affected the personal data of others, like faculty or other students, then the school sometimes blocks access to keep others' privacy from being compromised."

"There's really nothing? Not even a photo? Any contact info?"

He put the paper down and looked at the monitor again. "Just a few brief notes about his resume, probably entered by admissions when he first applied for entrance."

"Does it say where he did his undergrad?"

Adam hesitated.

"Please. They might have some way of reaching him. I really want to do this for Carlo."

"State University at Tarrytown."

Leila reached over and touched his wrist, his sticky skin repellent under her fingertips. "Thank you."

"Of course." Adam patted her hand again. "Of course."

She turned to go, paused.

"Remember when I won the school competition?"

"Still one of the best performances of the Rachmaninoff Second I ever heard."

"Thanks. Do you have the list of people who participated that year?"

Adam laughed. "Why would you want that?"

Participation in the conservatory's competition was by invitation only and the entire process, including each contestant's performance, was closed to the public. A dozen students total were handpicked by their teachers from all departments and one of the requirements for participation included silence.

The school imposed the gag policy to keep the already intensely competitive atmosphere among students in check. Only the winner was announced and no other prizes were awarded.

Even the judges voted independently without sharing their decisions. A winner was declared from the majority vote. If there was no majority, the judges discussed their picks until they reached one.

"Just a silly idea." Leila tucked a lock of hair behind her ear and waved her hand. "Forget it. I probably shouldn't have said anything —"

"Wait." Adam leaned in, his eyes wide. "What is it?"

"My parents are thinking of starting a music festival next summer. Nothing big," she lifted a shoulder, "a concert series plus workshops and masterclasses for students who audition. I thought it'd be nice to ask a few top alumni to play and teach for a few weeks. You know, old classmates teaching the next generation type of thing."

"That sounds exciting."

"No one knows about it yet." She gave a conspiratorial smile. "And I know those lists are not usually made public, but I thought winning it might cut me a bit of slack."

He beamed, pleased with the reminder he was associating with a winner. "I'll get a copy for you."

While Adam retrieved the list, Leila's phone pinged with a new message from Joshua.

Have meeting I can't get out of so can't meet you before concert. Will u be ok?

Nervous energy leaked through the words. Leila quickly wrote back:

Yes. Don't worry. See you after concert is over.

His reply came back a few seconds later.

U will be fantastic!!

"Here you go." Adam handed over a folded sheet of paper.

Leila murmured her thanks, exited through the school's main entrance, and stopped near the stairs leading to the plaza.

She opened the paper and scanned the list of names.

As she'd suspected, Robert Wynford was one of the participants. But another familiar name also leaped out at her from the middle of the page.

Sayaka Tanikawa.

Leila had assumed the murderer sent over Sayaka's underwear to highlight her relationship with Carlo. But what if it was something else?

Once again, the black and white photo of their frozen smiles flashed before her: Marlene, Paul, Helen, Heinrich, Anastasia, Elliot, and Vladimir.

And Leila, dangling in front, a fruit ripe for picking.

Despite yesterday's snow turning the ground slick with grey mush, the grand entrance of Avery Fisher Hall and the soaring arches of the Metropolitan Opera conveyed a steadfast decadence.

Orion waited for her by the fountain in his usual attire of worn jeans, sweater, and black coat, his hands shoved deep into his pockets.

Balanced on the balls of his feet, he stood with shoulders tensed, his gaze darting across faces like a prize fighter preparing for battle in the middle of a palace.

He watched her approach, his eyes on her the whole way, his face carrying a look of faint suspicion as if anything between 63rd and 65th weren't real.

"Thanks for meeting me," she said.

They sat along the fountain's edge, blending with the crowds of tourists, students, and artists.

"Have you checked out the names yet?"

Orion shook his head. "Your lawyer's been giving us a hard time. Supposed to be sending it over some time today."

Leila had given Brian a list of everyone she knew who'd ever been in her apartment. He was also supposed to have gathered a list from her parents.

The Ansonia had far too much security for anyone to have broken in. Whoever took Leila's underwear was someone who was invited in.

"Once we get it we'll start running them down, see if anyone also shows up on the hall security tapes."

"Anything new on Booth Hill Institute?"

Internet searches had yielded only a few vague mentions on outdated sites.

"Ian went to Tarrytown yesterday to check it out. It's a retirement home."

"What?"

"Rich old people taken care of by a big, fancy staff. You've never heard of it?"

Leila shook her head.

"He asked around but couldn't find any connection to you or your family." Orion rested his elbows on his knees, looking like he needed a cigarette. "Doesn't feel right."

"What doesn't?"

"All of it," he murmured, his gaze flickering over the performance halls, the melting sludge on the ground. "What do you know about Charlotte Russell?"

"The programming director? She doesn't like me much. Probably wanted me off the concert after the last rehearsal. Why?"

Orion took a moment to answer. "I think she's lying about something but I don't know what."

"Dealing with big egos can be stressful. I'm sure she's always lying about something." Leila hesitated, then handed him the folded paper. "Maybe this will help."

"What is it?"

"The photo on the music stand was taken four years ago when I won the school competition. That's a list of other people who also competed that year."

Orion scanned the sheet, stopping about halfway down. Leila turned away.

"She was out drinking with friends that night," he said quietly. "Several witnesses confirmed it."

Leila forced her brain to work past the betrayal still choking her throat. "How do you think they got her underwear?"

"Perp probably returned to Carlo's studio to grab it after we left and before my guys showed up. Carlo had quite a collection."

Leila knew what she should do: rest, run through the Brahms, prepare herself mentally and emotionally for the concert of her life, and leave death to people like Orion who made detective before the age of thirty.

But deep in her soul, she felt an unpleasant certainty.

If she didn't find out the truth now, she would never be able to walk away from Carlo.

She would't understand who she'd been with him and who she was now without him.

She wouldn't be able to make music.

"What is it?" Orion asked.

It was too early to tell him about Robert Wynford.

He had to narrow down possible suspects, go through the lists and spot the liar.

She had to follow the music.

"I think I want to check a few more things out," she said slowly. "We can talk after the concert tonight."

She'd need to hurry if she wanted to make it back in time.

"Be careful." Orion handed over his card. "You'll let me know as soon as you find something?"

Leila pocketed his number and stood. The lies that had come so easily all morning, once again slipped through her lips, light and smooth.

"Of course," she said.

****

Grand Central bustled with Friday lunchtime traffic, a mass of people flowing through the cavernous space like blood through the city's main artery.

Leila pocketed her train ticket, quickly moving aside for the next person behind her.

She glanced at the large four-faced clock topping the information booth. There wouldn't be enough time to stop at her apartment on the way back. She'd have to go directly to the hall.

Leila took out her phone and reluctantly called the only person who could help.

"Are you calling to explain why you didn't come to dinner last night?" Helen's voice crackled, bright and hard. "Your father is very disappointed. You know Craig is an important business associate."

Leila stepped outside the stream of crowds. "I needed to rest for today."

"I can barely hear you. What is that noise? Where are you?"

"Mom, I won't have time to grab my dress and things before the concert —"

"What are you talking about?"

"Can you have someone bring it to the hall? Everything is packed in the usual bag in my room."

"Leila." An edge entered her voice. "What's going on?"

"Nothing. I'm just outside, clearing my head."

"Why? Brian said you needed to stay inside. You've already caused enough trouble —"

"I didn't ask for this —"

"—and it's bad enough you had that ridiculous public spat with Carlo but now with the police crawling all over our apartment? It's *unseemly*, Leila. We've worked too hard to get you to this point."

"Not we."

"What?"

"We didn't work hard. I did."

"What is wrong with you? Getting you here required all of us. Tonight is just as much about your father and me as it is about you. Honestly, Leila, you don't know half the things I need to deal with before your concert, including any of screw-ups with the reception. And now I'll have to find someone to bring over your things."

A group of musicians soldiered across the main concourse, violins and cellos strapped to their bodies like armor.

"I gotta go." Leila hung up before Helen could reply.

A familiar blonde, her violin case bouncing against her hip, brought up the rear of the group. She turned to look at the display board and caught Leila's gaze.

Alexis halted, said something to the others.

Leila dipped her head, a dark curtain of hair concealing most of her face, and walked in the opposite direction toward her platform.

"Wait!"

Leila walked faster.

"I need to ask you something!"

Leila heard the barely suppressed fear in Alexis' voice, something that reminded her of that night in the dark Maine waters, thrashing and treading and sucking in air while the cold unknown yanked at her. She stopped.

"Did you tell the police I killed Carlo?"

Alexis was paler than the last time they'd spoken. Dark shadows ringed her eyes and Leila had an image of her wilting, her long limbs and blonde hair shrinking and pulling in to her hollow chest.

"You really think I killed him?"

"Doesn't matter what I think."

"There's a detective." Alexis watched the group of musicians head up the escalator, then looked back at her. "He questioned me. Called me again, wants to talk more."

Leila remained silent, both pleased and surprised Orion had kept pushing.

"I think he thinks I did it. He thinks I actually did something to Carlo —"

"That's not my problem."

Desperation wafted off Alexis, tangling with the nauseating scent of her perfume. "Everybody knows it was you. But you're using your family, your money, to put it on me."

Leila stepped away. "Don't fucking blame me for your guilt."

"I know what really happened between you and Carlo."

Leila turned back.

Alexis crossed her arms, triumph sparking in her washed-out eyes. "I know what was going on between you, him, and Charlotte."

"What are you talking about?"

"Carlo was leaving you. He didn't want to keep dragging you around with him. I saw them, day before he…" she swallowed, "day before what happened. Carlo and Charlotte were having lunch and I heard them say your name."

"So? They were probably talking about the concert —"

"Then why did they get quiet as soon as they saw me?" Her face pinched, mouth tightening, cheeks drawing in. "They were going to cut you out of this concert and future tour dates. That's why you did it."

"No one's going to believe that."

"We'll see." Alexis straightened. "If you try to pin this on me, I'll tell the cops what I know and not even your Cates money will be able to help you."

She strode away, her height and swaying hips drawing attention as she crossed the main concourse.

It would've been easier to reject Alexis' bizarre accusation if Leila hadn't felt a kernel of truth to it.

She boarded the Metro-North train, thinking about Carlo's library of photos and string of one-night stands.

Orion said the only woman he'd stayed with for more than one night was Alexis. Had Carlo's lies extended past personal betrayal into professional ones as well?

The overcast sky thickened as the train sped north along the Hudson, cloaking Tarrytown in a grey fog.

From the train station, Leila took a cab, the drive showcasing a charming, picturesque town nestled in the heart of the Hudson Valley.

Booth Hill Institute was located on a secluded multi-acre park along the river. The large Gothic building, its brick walls dark with moisture, appeared in the misty haze like a giant beast looming over the town.

Leila spoke to the pleasant receptionist sitting behind a large, marble counter. The head nurse would be down shortly to answer her questions.

Behind her, two ornate staircases gracefully arced up to the upper floors. Mahogany, marble, and parquet steeped the building in an hushed, old world elegance that spoke of money and class.

The faint strains of Chopin's melancholic refrain reached her ears and Leila followed the music down the hall on her right to a large recreation room.

A dozen elderly men and women occupied couches and tables in the elegantly furnished space. Some played chess or Yahtzee, others read quietly or laughed with one of the smiling orderlies.

It didn't feel like a retirement home; it felt like a five-star vacation home for seniors.

A tiny woman with silvery hair played on a Baldwin baby grand piano tucked into the back corner.

Leila gravitated toward the music, listening to her play with a nimbleness belying her age.

Wrinkled fingers crossed the keyboard, drawing out the familiar lilting melody of Chopin's Second Nocturne. The tempo was slow, very slow, but there was enough flow to recognize she'd once been a solid pianist.

The final *ritardando* to the end was graceful and as she slowly released the pedal, the last chord dissipated into the air like a ghost.

Several people applauded. Leila joined them.

The old woman turned.

"Hello," she said pleasantly. "What's your name?"

"Leila."

"I'm Rita."

"It's nice to meet you. I really enjoyed your performance."

"Do you like music?"

Leila smiled. "I do. I love music. I love Chopin."

"Oh, it's my favorite nocturne." She glanced down at her hands, dotted with dark brown spots. "I used to play it much better."

"I thought it was beautiful." Leila pulled out a chair and sat beside her. "Were you a musician?"

"Oh, no, no. But my mother made me take lessons and I enjoyed it." She tenderly ran those wrinkled fingers over the keys. "It takes many, many hours of practice to play them."

"I know."

Rita smiled. "But my boy. He's a musician, you know. He practiced hard and became a wonderful artist."

Leila felt that certainty again, a hard awareness that told her this was what she'd been searching for all along, a truth that went beyond art or logic or Carlo's murder and was already embedded deep inside her.

"What does he play?"

Rita rubbed her fingers over the black keys as if cleaning dirt off them.

"What kind of musician is your son?" Leila leaned in. "Does he play an instrument?"

Rita turned back to her and laughed, a tinkling bright sound that belonged to a young girl.

"I don't have a son." She dropped her voice to a whisper. "But Benjamin might propose soon and I think I'm going to say yes."

Leila hid her disappointment. "That would be nice. Do you love

Benjamin?"

Rita giggled, covering her mouth with both hands, eyes shining like stars on a canvas wrinkled with time.

"Maybe," she said coyly. "He's very charming and he'll only dance with me."

"Hello. You must be Leila." A slender woman in her sixties approached, her hair neatly pinned back, every inch of her pressed attire screaming of controlled efficiency. "I'm Beth Sanders, the head nurse here."

"Nice to meet you."

Beth lightly touched Rita's shoulder. "Did you play the piano for our guest?"

"She loves Chopin. Like me." Rita beamed up at Leila. "Isn't he simply romantic?"

Leila nodded, unsure if she were still speaking about Benjamin.

Rita wrapped those bony hands with the twisted muscles and dotted skin around Leila's slim fingers.

The two hands, old and young, curved over the piano keys, the bridge of their knuckles forming a perfect arc as if they held invisible fruit in their palms.

"My boy, Elliot," she said somberly. "He's a good boy."

Milky grey eyes stared at Leila with the same intensity as a parishioner kneeling in a confessional, baring their sins to their priest or God, seeking forgiveness and absolution.

"I'm sure he is," Leila said softly.

"Ms. Frank," Beth said. "Lewis is looking for you again. You don't want to miss your favorite show."

"Yes, yes." Rita stood from the piano with a look of delight.

Beth watched her carefully make her way to an old man with an oxygen tank sitting in front of a large television.

"Sometimes she's lucid, sometimes she's not."

"Has she been here long?"

"Almost four years now. We do what we can to keep her comfortable, but some days are better than others."

"Did you say her name was Frank? She's Rita Frank?"

Beth nodded.

"And she has a son named Elliot?"

"Yes, he comes to visit her once a month. Do you know the family?"

"No," Leila murmured, her hands turning to ice. "I must've mistaken her for someone else."

She accompanied Beth out to the main lobby. While the head nurse talked excitedly about the facilities and staff, Leila walked beside her with unseeing eyes, her mind turning everything over this way and that, analyzing pieces in the same way she considered each phrase in a score.

It took a few moments for her to realize Beth had stopped.

"I'm sorry?"

"The receptionist said you might be interested in bringing your grandmother?" Beth asked. "I know these things are difficult to consider, much less prepare for, but I've been here for forty years and I deeply believe Booth Hill provides the best possible care."

Leila touched the stair banister, took in the vaulted ceilings. "I was actually referred here by a family friend. Maybe you know them? The Wynfords?"

Beth stiffened. "Of course. Janet Wynford worked here for over thirty years."

"That's right." Leila nodded. "Her son, Robert, referred me here."

Beth stepped back, widening the distance between them. "What happened was hard for everyone. How's Robert doing?"

"Good, good. Does he ever come here to visit?"

"Not after Janet passed."

"Oh, right." Leila shifted, her mind twisting, turning. "How long has it been already?"

"Well, she left four years ago, so it's been about tw—"

"Two years. Time goes by so fast."

"Yes," Beth said, impatient. "Do you have any other questions?"

"Do you have a brochure? Maybe a cost sheet I could take a look at?"

"Of course." Her voice turned frosty. "My receptionist will get that for you."

"Thank you."

Beth gave a sharp nod and left to attend patients and families who would never do anything so gauche as to ask about money.

Armed with a brochure featuring images of attractive senior citizens wearing wide smiles that showed off their dentures, Leila called a cab and returned to the train station.

She settled into her seat on the train, the photo on the music stand hammering at her. Besides Vladimir, the three other judges were also highly esteemed artists in their respective fields.

Heinrich Descher was one of the most respected composers alive. He'd also been Robert Wynford's teacher at Juilliard. Anastasia Rossen, a world-renowned mezzo-soprano, was now retired. But at the time of the competition, she was a powerful force to be reckoned with at the Metropolitan Opera.

Then there was Elliot Frank, who had been Sayaka's teacher. A protégé of Rostropovich, the cellist was on SMI's roster and had a major solo career. His ailing mother was also living in an exclusive, high-priced facility, the kind of place a cellist - no matter how well-known - couldn't afford.

Her phone buzzed with a call from the New York Philharmonic's manager. She declined it.

Dress rehearsal had already begun. If there were no delays, she'd arrive at the hall about an hour before the concert. Leila wondered if the orchestra would run through the Brahms concerto without her, play the grand *tutti* sections with the same inevitability she felt as the train glided along the curves of the river.

She picked up her phone and called a number she thought she'd never use.

"Didn't expect to hear from you so soon."

Hector's voice snaked through the lines, tickling her ear with an uncomfortably intimate tone.

"It's an emergency."

"I'm listening."

"You know the school server inside out, right?"

She heard a shuffle, a few bags shifting around. "Maybe."

"There's a sealed student file I need to access."

"You want the whole thing?"

"No. Just his photo. Can you text it over as soon as you have it?"

"Sure. What's the name?"

"Robert Wynford." She spelled it out.

"Okay." She heard rustling paper. "I'll take care of this as soon as the performance is over."

"Wait. You're playing a concert right now?"

"We're in intermission." She heard his amused smile. "Mendelssohn trio in the second half. Soon as that's done, I'll get this for you."

He emphasized the last two words a bit, making sure she understood payment would be due eventually.

"Thanks."

Her next message was to Orion.

May know who later today but don't know why yet.

Meet @ hall after concert.

She sent the text.

Her phone buzzed again, angry and insistent.

Outside, the river flashed by in a steady rhythm, ice coating the surface in a dull, metallic sheen and freezing the churning waters beneath.

TEN

Leila hurried through the hall's back entrance, pre-concert energy buzzing around her, hot and electric.

Orchestra musicians stopped in mid-stride, whispers racing through the hall about her swollen jaw and disheveled hair.

Leila saw and heard none of it.

She was used to hectic touring schedules and last-minute performance changes, her mind disciplined over the years to snap into performance-level focus at will.

It was an hour before the concert. More than enough time to warm up her fingers and double-check acoustics before changing and getting ready.

Between the curtains on stage right, she caught a glimpse of the piano, lid open wide, positioned for the dress rehearsal she'd missed. A few orchestra musicians still remained on stage, practicing.

Leila tuned out the dissonance of the other instruments and focused on the black and white keys gleaming beneath the lights.

A violinist stood, providing a clear view of the conductor's podium and the floor between Alexis' chair and the piano bench.

The intense, narrow concentration she'd honed over the years slipped out of her control and greedily latched on to something else.

It bored into that small area between soloist and orchestra leader, yanking forward memories of that patch of stage saturated with crimson, pink flecks of tissue and brains caught in the thick flow.

Leila stared, feet glued to the ground, breathing in the scents of overripe fruit and death, feeling that blood taint the stage, taint her instrument, relentlessly dragging her attention away from her life and back to his death.

The violinist exiting the stage shouldered her.

"Finally decided to show up?" he muttered.

Leila blinked. Nothing but a bleached, sterile floor and two stagehands approaching the piano.

She forced her legs to move. "Wait!"

The older stagehand, a man in his fifties with a flat, bored expression, said, "We gotta roll it off."

The Brahms was the second piece on the program, after a brief Mozart overture.

"I just need a minute. Please."

He looked at the other stagehand and shrugged. "A minute."

"Thank you."

They headed off and Leila settled at the piano, ignoring the glares of the others on stage.

She'd lost the orchestra in her last rehearsal with Carlo; skipping today's rehearsal had crushed any chance of fixing that.

They would never trust her, never play with her in the way necessary to create a performance of true cohesion.

But Leila no longer cared.

She simply wanted to play her Brahms, unhindered by others.

Leila began, her sight, hearing, and touch simultaneously focused on the instrument before her and the space around her.

Vladimir had taught her to listen on three different levels when performing with an orchestra: she needed to hear herself, hear what the audience heard, and what the orchestra heard.

This way of working - her ears listening from a variety of perspectives, processing sensory input while her fingers readjusted every millisecond, sensitive to the speed and weight necessary to produce exactly the right sound on exactly the right note - was a result of the levers and pulleys operating in Leila's mind.

She ran through a larger, trickier passage in the third movement, her fingers loosening up, awakening muscles stiff from the cold.

But it was difficult to find her space, the place where music poured from her, natural and easy.

Being on this stage provided a terrible temptation. Her mind wanted to look, to return to that spot between her and the podium in the same way the ping of her father's phone yanked his attention away like a Pavlovian experiment.

Muscle memory kicked in and her fingers effortlessly flew across the keys, fueled by the hundreds and thousands of hours she'd dedicated to learning and practicing this piece.

But she couldn't find the music.

"Miss." The stagehand stopped beside her, rested his arm on the music stand. "We really need to get this off stage. The hall is opening in a few minutes."

"Oh. Of course."

Leila stood, watched them carefully push the eight-foot Steinway off stage right, the wheels silently rolling, rolling across that bleached, sterile floor.

Swallowing back her uncertainty, she headed backstage and was accosted by a furious Frenchman.

"How dare you."

René Chaveau's concert tuxedo meticulously fit his slim frame and he somehow managed to portray immaculate style and nothing of substance all at the same time.

Sandy brown hair flopped over his eyes and he tossed his head back, his face pale with indignation.

"This is absolutely unprofessional." Distress elongated his vowels, strengthening his French accent. "You would leave me here, like an idiot in front of the orchestra —"

"I'm sorry. There were problems on the train —"

"I do not care where you were." He tossed his arms up. "I cannot imagine anyone sacrificing the last rehearsal before their debut. You are not serious. Not an artist."

"It'll be fine," Leila kept her voice calm, sensible. "I've toured with this concerto for months now. All you have to do is follow me —"

"*Excuse-moi?* Follow you?" His voice rose. He smoothed back his hair, touched his cufflinks as if to assure himself nothing had flown out of place. "That will never happen."

Leila, still feeling unbalanced from the stage, held up her hand. "I'm the soloist —"

"A soloist who doesn't respect her orchestra. No one will follow you. They will follow me." He shook his head. "I do not care who you are Miss Cates. I do not care about you Americans and your money and whoever your family is. I care about art. And you do not deserve to play on this stage with this orchestra when you care so little for it."

Leila's mind struggled to respond, the edges still sticky with that blood, with the stage's hunger.

"You didn't even want to perform tonight."

"What are you talking about?" Rene straightened his arms again, touched both sleeves on his wrist, and craned his neck to look at the stage.

"You didn't want to fill in. Was it too last minute? Were you afraid —"

"I don't know what you are talking about, but this is my debut with this orchestra." He buttoned his tuxedo, paused, then unbuttoned it again. "Carlo never let me guest conduct and if he hadn't died, there was no way I'd ever …" He stopped, his gaze flickering to Leila. "My condolences," he muttered. "But I would be an idiot to turn this down, no?"

He marched away, his slim figure straight as a lance.

Leila needed to think, get her mind under control and calm her shaky insides.

The sounds from the hall swelled and she peeked around the curtain, watched the audience flow through rows and aisles and take their seats.

She wouldn't let Carlo take this from her, dead or alive.

But when Leila reached her dressing room, a tall, slender shadow awaited her.

"Hi."

Sayaka stepped forward, face pale and eyes dark beneath the muted lights.

"I know once you enter, you won't come back out until the concert. I just wanted to wish you good luck and tell you that I think you're going to play great."

An awkward silence descended.

Sayaka looked down, then at the wall just above Leila's shoulder. A sparkly barrette clipped her hair back and the light played across it, pulling an image from Leila's memory.

Sayaka turned to go.

"Did a composer named R. Wynford write something for you?"

She looked back. "What?"

"Someone sent you a suite for solo cello and you hated it."

"Yeah. Yeah, can't remember his name, though. Hang on. I have the e-mail he sent me." Sayaka pulled out her phone and scrolled, the screen's light casting her face in an otherworldly glow.

Her finger stopped. "Robert Wynford."

There was a moment when Leila knew something she was working on was ready to be performed.

It was when everything felt exactly right, technique and artistry working together - not against each other - to form one cohesive idea.

That same lever now slid into place in Leila's mind and all the disparate pieces fit together with an audible click.

She needed confirmation.

She needed, of all people, Hector.

"Did Wynford send that package to your apartment?" Sayaka asked.

Leila opened the dressing room door.

"Who is he?"

Just like with Alexis, it was the undercurrent of fear in her voice that stopped Leila. She didn't want to tell her. She wanted Sayaka to wonder, to worry a little while longer, live with the uncertainty that Leila had drowned in over the past few days.

She couldn't do it.

"Four years ago, he participated in the conservatory competition. The one I won." Leila faced her. "The one you also competed in."

Sayaka leaned against the wall, chin tucked in, arms wrapped around her stomach. She didn't bother denying it.

"Did you recognize the photo on the music stand? The one that was sent to my house?"

She nodded. "That was when they officially announced you as the winner."

"Why didn't you tell me you entered the competition?"

"We weren't supposed to tell."

"I told you."

Leila had talked to her about it almost everyday, bitching about practice, speculating about the other competitors, working through the nerves and anxiety.

Not once had Sayaka mentioned she was participating, too.

She dropped her head. "I don't know why. Maybe I was scared. Elliot thought I might have a chance."

"But—"

"But I wasn't good enough to try for a solo career?" Sayaka glanced up, her voice tight.

"No, I thought you weren't interested in one."

"Elliot thought I had a shot at it," she evaded. "It's harder for a cellist. You know that."

Leila nodded.

"If I had any chance at attracting attention, it was though the competition."

But Leila had won and Sayaka had taken an orchestra job, a steady position with benefits and a union, so long as you were willing to be swallowed up by the group.

"Is that why you were with Carlo?"

"Leila, you're about to perform. It's not the right time."

"You don't get to decide that."

Sayaka exhaled, dropped her head back. "When you won, I was happy for you. I really was. I always figured that competition was like a sign, you know? If I was meant for the solo stuff, I'd win. And if I didn't," she shrugged, "it wasn't meant to be. But a year later, you got together with Carlo and it was like…"

"Like what?"

"It was like everything changed. I mean, now you were with Belandini, a superstar." She straightened and for a moment, her eyes were as hard and flat as Marlene's. "You were getting everything - the competition, the career, the agent, the famous boyfriend to help you - served to you on a platter, Leila, like you always do."

Leila's legs shook a little. "And?"

"And nothing." Sayaka sagged, the momentary hardness vanishing. "We'd all gone out one night and you left early because you had to get up for a rehearsal the next day. Carlo and I started talking and I got really hammered and…" She looked at her. "It was a horrible mistake, Leila. Even if tell you how sorry I am, I know it'll never make up for what I did. But that's all it was. One drunken night when I made a stupid, stupid mistake."

A mistake. Classical musicians weren't supposed to make them.

Leila managed a nod. "Now I know."

Sayaka faltered. "Leila —"

She entered the dressing room and closed the door behind her.

A Chanel gown hung neatly on the clothing rack; her makeup, jewelry, and hair styling tools were arranged across the vanity. The usual backstage package from SMI awaited her on the coffee table: two bottles of her favorite wine, a dark chocolate bar, a bottle of water, and a plate of fresh fruits.

Leila downed a glass of wine with shaking hands and devoured half the chocolate bar before beginning her preparations.

Later, as she sat at the dressing table, the Brahms score open before her, bound tight in a dress slightly too small with her face painted a little too much, Leila wondered when she'd become this person who padded herself from the truth like her mother, insulating herself with costumes, music, and alcohol.

She glanced again at her phone. It remained motionless and quiet.

Mozart filled the room, the music coming from speakers mounted on the corners. The orchestra was nearing the end of the opening overture, strings crescendoing to the final climax.

A knock at the door. "Ms. Cates, it's time."

Leila took her phone and handkerchief and followed the stage manager through the darkened corridors to the waiting area off stage right.

The overture ended with a snappy flourish and the hall erupted in warm applause.

René walked off stage, red patches of exhilaration dotting his pasty skin.

"The audience is electric." He straightened his arms, smoothed his bow tie. "It will be an unforgettable night. I feel it."

He mopped the sweat at his brow with his handkerchief and strode out to soak in the applause.

René stepped back on to the podium, his movements crisp and fast, and the clapping politely came to an end.

Her phone buzzed.

Leila opened Hector's text and clicked the image preview.

Stagehands wheeled the piano out from the opposite side of the stage, positioned it, and exited.

An expectant hush settled over the hall.

The image began to download at an excruciating pace, slowed by poor cell phone service.

"Any time, Ms. Cates," the stage manager murmured.

Forty percent downloaded.

A few coughs from the audience. René faced her from the podium, hands clasped in front of him, brows furrowed.

"Ms. Cates."

Sixty percent.

Whispered murmurs now joined the coughing fits.

René glared, a purple flush crawling up his thin neck.

"Ms. Cates, you have to go. Now."

"One second."

Come on, come on.

The image finished downloading, filling the screen with a familiar face.

René stepped off the podium.

"Go!"

The stage manager yanked the phone from her with one hand and pushed her hard with the other.

Leila stumbled, then found her footing.

René waited beside the podium, his brows raised so high, they disappeared under his limp hair.

Leila walked out, mind reeling, arms and chest numb, the audience's applause muffled and distant.

She bowed and settled at the piano, giving the keys one last swipe before tucking her handkerchief into the frame.

Leila looked over her shoulder. Alexis ignored her.

Leila nodded at René. He gave an ingratiating smile and turned to the orchestra.

Her ears caught every detail: the rustle of clothing, the crinkle of a program. Leila focused on her heartbeat, willing it to slow and match her breaths, and shoved that image on her phone to the deepest recesses of her mind.

René lifted his baton.

She closed her eyes.

Listened.

A collective inhale…and the music began.

The lush opening unfurled, narrating an epic saga of passion and yearning. René's tempo was moderate, not the grand slow pomposity Carlo favored or the passionate drive Leila wanted.

It was safe, an acceptable and pleasing interpretation that wouldn't ruffle anyone's feathers.

It was also terrible, as bland and forgettable as the new music scores she'd dismissed.

The piano entered the story, bringing a new voice to the narrative. Her fingers brushed the keys, her heart straining to find satisfaction in the harmonic shifts and subtle colorings.

It wasn't there.

Leila closed her eyes, tried new ways of speaking a phrase - holding back, pushing forward, adding an unexpected accent, waiting a breath before the harmonic resolution.

But she couldn't find it.

She pushed the music forward with frantic exhilaration, dragging the orchestra behind her.

René shot her a warning look.

Leila drove hard, demanding they follow, viciously attacking the finale as she searched for what eluded her.

But when the last chord exploded, ringing with a rage composed of love and longing, Leila felt nothing but a drained emptiness.

It was as if the reins keeping her in control, in the carefully constructed environment where she'd always created music, had snapped and broken away.

Everything had felt just beyond reach. The notes had danced before her but she'd been unable to grasp them, to own and mold them into what she wanted to say.

"Brava!"

Leila blinked.

People stood, flooding the hall with a deluge of approval for her sacrifice on stage.

René's eyes glittered with triumph. He joined the thunderous applause and Leila was unsure if he was clapping for her or for himself for making it through.

Sayaka met her gaze, the corners of her mouth turned up in a small, tremulous smile.

Numb, Leila stood, smiled at no one, gave a small half-nod to the sea of shadows and walked off.

The applause grew into a voracious roar.

It didn't matter if Leila had nothing to give.

The audience demanded it, the stage demanded it.

"Encore!"

"Brava!"

The stage manager waited for her to make her decision.

Leila hesitated, then walked back to the piano with unseeing eyes.

Satisfied, the audience settled back in their seats.

Hungry eyes watched her. Waited.

Leila stared at the keys.

She didn't know what to play.

René shifted on the podium, gave her a nervous glance.

Leila rested her fingers on the keys.

It started hesitant and translucent, a simple story about entering a dream and exploring the unknown with a child's innocence.

But as she continued to play Schumann's *Träumerei*, the colors darkened, no longer the limpid purity of a child's tale, but an adult truth of death and lies.

The last note ended in a quiet rasp, a whispery promise both painful and alluring.

This time, the applause was louder, greedier.

Leila hurried off stage and shook her head at the stage manager.

She closed the door of her dressing room, her pulse racing hot beneath her cold skin, hands shaking uncontrollably.

The music was gone and Leila couldn't help but feel as if Carlo had shattered and stolen her faith, taken her voice with him when he died and left behind an emptiness she no longer knew how to fill.

Leila had spent so much time fighting the current, struggling to keep her head above water and maintain the life she had, without realizing she'd already been swept past the point of no return.

By the time her trembling eased, the beginning measures of Strauss had begun drifting through the speakers. Intermission was already over.

Orion. She had to tell him about the image Hector sent.

Leila searched her bag, the vanity, the bathroom for her phone, remembering too late that the stage manager had taken it from her before she performed.

When the door opened behind her, she knew.

The truth had finally come calling and there was nowhere left to hide.

Not behind Carlo. Not behind the Cates name.

And not behind the piano.

The face she knew entered and said:

"How does it feel to fail?"

ELEVEN

The door closed with a soft click.

Strauss' *Tod und Verklärung* filled the space between them, a dark, restless *agitato* of horns and strings.

"The audience asked for an encore," Leila said. "How is that a failure?"

"There's a difference between success and spectacle. The first movement was a disjointed mess. You were ahead of the orchestra the entire second movement and you ignored René in the recapitulation. It's a miracle he didn't have a heart attack."

A gun, outfitted with a silencer, gleamed in his gloved hands.

Joshua nodded at her. "Against the table."

Leila slowly backed up, eyes on him, until her hip bumped against the vanity.

"You're Robert Wynford."

He limped, his left foot lightly touching the ground, staring at her hands as if he wanted to crush them.

"I was," he corrected. "I changed my name after I left Juilliard. New name, new life."

At their last meeting, he'd concealed his injury, his rage, by remaining seated behind his desk and its cluster of delicate crystal figurines, sparkling like Sayaka's barrette.

"But you still composed. You wrote for Sayaka and me. Solo works for cello and piano."

"It's not as if you looked at it, Leila." He sat on the sofa arm, gun pointed at her the entire time. "But appropriate don't you think? New compositions dedicated to the person who ended my career and another one of your victim."

"Is that why you went over to Carlo's studio? To find something on Sayaka?"

"Oh, Carlo had hidden all sorts of things, but I thought hers would have the most impact. I admit, it wasn't my first time there." He smiled at her expression. "Marlene had a spare key for their occasional rendezvous."

Joshua had always been forgettable, something about him fading around the edges and blending into the background, a quality that made it easy to ignore his calls and texts.

Leila was no longer sure if Robert Wynford, the composer, had always been that way or if Joshua Levinson, SMI agent, had exploited it to pursue his agenda.

She remembered the pile of scores in Carlo's studio, the twinkling conductor's baton on Joshua's desk.

"You also wrote something for him." She tucked her hands behind her. "A symphonic work."

"A tone poem for orchestra. Inspired by the works of Dante and Petrarch."

The strings crescendoed, the rich, soaring theme pouring through the speakers.

That was why Joshua had joined SMI. He'd wanted to get inside, network with enough musicians and presenters to make inroads for his compositions.

Joshua had always pushed his artists to premiere contemporary works, handing them score after score, talking about music with that zealous glint in his eye.

"Marlene didn't know about my compositions. Of course, she doesn't much about anything." His uninjured leg bounced up and down. "She just wanted someone who actually knew music and could tell her all the right things to say."

Leila leaned back, slid her fingers across the table and brushed against something hard.

"Carlo didn't deserve to die."

"People like you and Carlo harm innocents."

"I don't know what he did, but I've never done anything to you, Josh."

His leg stopped bouncing. "Thousands of pianists graduate from conservatories across the world every year. Do you really think you could've landed a contract with SMI and this debut at your age, without your mother working behind the scenes?"

She stopped moving her fingers.

Joshua tilted his head. "Oh you poor, deluded thing. You really did."

Her throat felt too tight. "You're lying."

"You can't escape who you are, Leila. You're a Cates."

No. She was a pianist, an artist.

She was not like her mother, frozen and hard, categorizing everything and everyone as either first-class or not. Or her father with his shiny smile, old boy's club, and benders of prostitutes and booze.

When she played, whether on stage or at home alone, she was no longer a Cates. She didn't have respect because of the size of her bank account or her name; she earned it because what she did at the keyboard was something no one else could do.

"Helen is on the board of Lincoln Center, Carnegie Hall, and the Tanglewood Festival," he said. "Do you honestly believe you won that Juilliard competition on your own?"

"Is that why you sent that photo?" Leila pulled the clasp, her fingers feeling their way through the small opening into her makeup bag. "Because you think I cheated?"

"I know you did."

Something cold and ugly twisted his face. Joshua stood, his torso bunching and tightening under his insipid suit, pointing the gun at her face and taking up all the air in the room.

"First judge, Elliot Frank. After the competition, his ailing mother, whom he was unable to care for, moves into the most luxurious, expensive facility in New York State."

The faint refrain of Chopin echoed in Leila's ears. "Booth Hill Institute."

"That's right." Joshua smiled. "You picked that up from the package I sent you. Smart girl."

"Your mother worked there."

"Two for two. That's also how I know Helen Cates was paying for Rita Frank's care." He paused. "My mother was fired after I filed a grievance with the school about the competition."

"You have no proof about any of this —"

"Anastasia was actually quite forthcoming, especially after enough alcohol."

Leila swallowed, her fingers searching through lipsticks and eyeshadow cases for the feel of cold metal.

"My family has nothing to do with that facility."

"Not officially. But several members of the Booth Hill board belong to the same clubs and charities as your parents." Joshua shrugged. "What's a small favor among friends? Getting rid of an older nurse nearing retirement was easy. Just have a fellow employee report she'd witnessed her stealing meds. Not hard to do."

It would also explain head nurse Beth's nervousness over the subject of Janet Wynford.

"Let's move on to the rest of the judging panel." Joshua half-limped, half- paced, the nervous energy trapped in his jittering legs shimmering up his torso, wiggling his dull blue tie.

Leila kept her gaze on Joshua and dug deeper inside the bag.

"Second judge, Anastasia Rossen."

"She voted against me."

Joshua halted. "And who told you that?"

Helen said Vladimir had mentioned it after the competition was over.

But votes were sealed. Vladimir couldn't have known how Anastasia voted.

Her mother shouldn't have had that information.

Joshua gave a smug smile and resumed his pseudo-pacing. "She thought Sayaka should've won. Do you know what happened after she voted against you?"

A scandal had erupted. Anastasia, an aging opera singer, had been making several of her male students sleep with her in exchange for parts at the Metropolitan Opera.

The story had broken in *Classical Music Today* and she'd been forced into retiring from the stage and left Juilliard.

"The threat of a Cates lawsuit, of course, keeps her from going to the press about it. Poor woman is now doing singing gigs at birthday parties." Disdain dripped off his voice. "Then of course, there's the third judge, Heinrich Descher. My teacher."

"I've never met him."

"Yes, because you refuse to learn any contemporary music," Joshua said, impatient. "If you did, you'd know that the year after the competition, Heinrich was appointed artistic director of one of the most important new music concert series in the world."

She remembered. "The Freiburg Festival."

"Whose biggest sponsor is AxitCorp."

Leila's stomach clenched at the mention of her father's company.

"And finally, we have Vladimir Markov."

One week ago, the idea that Vladimir would compromise his artistic integrity and throw a competition was unthinkable.

There is no worse fate for an artist than being forgotten, Leila.

Joshua stopped. "You know, don't you?"

Vladimir had taught her, guided her, made Leila feel as if she belonged to his world of great artists, to the stories he told over vodka.

"Helen promised Vladimir his career back," Joshua continued. "And Marlene agreed to help."

His recent performances, his upcoming concert in Prague.

"Well, officially, Marlene would never put Vladimir back on the SMI roster because of the booze. I mean there's only so far she's willing to go."

Helen's words in the cab ride the night of Carlo's death drifted through

Leila's mind.

Even Marlene has her limits.

"But she feeds Vladimir enough work that his ego is satisfied and he feels like something more than a teacher."

"Why would Marlene help him?" Leila heard the quiver in her voice. "Why would she do what my mother says? She's rich, she doesn't need —"

"Because Helen threatened to blacklist SMI and all its artists," Joshua said patiently as if explaining to a child. "Lincoln Center, Carnegie, Tanglewood. All her European contacts. You don't understand how powerful Helen's charitable acts make her. Your mother could easily bring down Marlene if she wanted to and there are other agencies and artists who'd be happy to fill in for SMI."

Leila heard the truth in his voice, knew it in the part of herself that lay buried beneath the countless hours of practice, the relentless dedication and single-minded focus.

It was easier to believe she'd earned success than to believe anything else had a factor in it.

It was the lie of the American Dream - work hard and you'll win, that poisonous mantra poured down the throat of every child, every teacher, every adult who wondered why they were still stuck in the same place after forty years of overtime, with nothing to show but bone-weary exhaustion, shitty health, and a pile of bills.

She'd swallowed the drug of potential, believed it, pinned her faith to it.

And she'd been just as delusional as Joshua in her adherence to it.

In reality she was part of the very machinery she'd mocked, the structure that kept musicians like Sayaka in a small, salaried position, a cog serving a larger purpose.

"The deal with Marlene didn't just end there, of course." Joshua settled on the sofa arm again. "Your SMI contract is contingent upon your parents paying the company a monthly retainer to keep you on the roster."

This was not what we agreed to.

Marlene and Helen had been talking about her as if she were a piece of property to be examined, scrutinized, and sold to the highest bidder.

"Pitiful, but certainly not the worst part."

"Stop," she whispered.

Joshua looked up, closed his eyes, listened as the full orchestra crescendoed into the final glorious climax leading to the moment of transcendent transfiguration.

Leila's fingers brushed against cold metal. She grasped the tiny scissors used for clipping loose threads off her gowns and carefully slid it out of the bag.

Joshua opened his eyes. "That's my favorite part. The final hours of an artist as he greets death."

She tucked the sharp object into her right hand, her long musician fingers wrapping around it.

Joshua pointed his gun at her chest. "Step away from the table."

She cautiously moved forward, pulse racing, hands buried in the folds of her gown.

He watched her with hard eyes for a moment longer, then lowered the gun.

"Poor Leila. Finding Alexis with Carlo was the great disaster of your coddled life, when there was so much more you didn't know."

"I know about the other women," she said flatly.

"Did you also know Marlene arranged for Carlo to meet your parents before he gave that first, memorable masterclass at Juilliard?"

Leila looked away, ice clumping in her chest.

Joshua gave a mock sigh. "How remarkable that a celebrated conductor fell in love at first sight with a student."

These were the answers she'd wanted, the ones Orion warned she'd never hear from Carlo's lips.

But she could hear them from Joshua.

"Did my mother arrange for that, too?"

Joshua smiled, pleased by the question. "Carlo needed funding for his larger projects, including recordings. Marlene wanted Carlo to have absolute support at all the large arts institutions. And Helen wanted her daughter to be a superstar." He shrugged. "Pretty ingenious when you think about it. In exchange for being with you and providing the media and exposure needed to boost your career, Carlo received money for all his projects as well as important guest conducting appearances with major orchestras."

"So you got back at me by killing him?"

Joshua dropped his shoulders, exhaled. "All he had to do was follow the plan, but those Italians..." he waved his hand, "too unpredictable."

Leila reviewed what had clicked in her mind before the performance, beginning with Carlo's words from their last rehearsal and the information Alexis had inadvertently provided.

I fought for you to have this concert when most resisted. She's too young, they said. A pianist of questionable talent.

He was going to leave you.

Carlo and Charlotte had lunch together a few days ago, and Joshua met with her on the night of his death.

"Charlotte didn't want me to play tonight," Leila said. "She spoke to Carlo and he was considering it because he was planning to leave me."

"Carlo was tired of being at Helen and Marlene's beck and call and Charlotte was pushing him hard. Since I'm your manager, he came to me for advice. Wanted to know what would be the best thing to do for you."

This clearly delighted Joshua to no end. He smiled and leaned forward, eager to tell the story.

"I told him I had my concerns because you were young and didn't seem very interested in building a serious career."

Leila gripped the silk folds of her gown, the scissor tip digging into her palm.

"He asked if I'd find some way to take you off the concert. Of course, he'd owe me."

Joshua shifted and the light sharpened his face, illuminated the cunning hidden behind his insurance salesman smile.

"I told him Heinrich needed someone to premiere an American symphonic work for his festival in Germany and I had a score I thought was perfect for it."

His Wynford work of art, the symphonic tone poems written especially for Carlo.

Joshua stood, his movements jerky.

Over the speakers, the orchestra had begun to diminuendo, the music reaching the final solemn measures chronicling an artist's death.

"When the Manhattan Chamber Ensemble concert ended, I entered the hall through the front and waited until Carlo arrived for his usual practice session."

That was why he hadn't appeared on the security footage covering the back entrance.

"Our meeting that night was supposed to be simple. Do you know how thrilling it was to hear about the rehearsal? Now Carlo had what he needed to dump your undeserving ass and all I had to do was reluctantly agree you weren't ready. He'd then premiere my work at the very festival my former traitorous teacher runs."

Punish Leila, mock his former teacher for betraying him, and gain Carlo Belandini as an important ally.

It was brilliant; except it didn't work out that way.

"Carlo refused to premiere your work."

"That idiot still wanted to perform the concert with you. Said he'd rather play with you, with all of your youthful anger, than conduct my piece."

The irony cut deep. Her relationship with Carlo had been an utter lie and he'd betrayed her countless times over the course of three years.

And yet with his last breath, he'd chosen her over Joshua and died for it, still clutching that Wynford symphonic masterpiece.

"He laughed and called it simplistic. A cheap homage." Joshua stilled, his body tightening with remembered fury.

Once again, someone had chosen Leila over him and it had sent Joshua spinning into an uncontrollable rage.

She'd been both right and wrong about the killer.

Robert Wynford was a composer, a musician.

But Joshua Levinson, the person who smashed the music stand into Carlo's head, wasn't a musician.

He was simply one of the countless others who'd been forgotten.

"But as I was leaving, Helen called, told me you were on your way and I realized how perfect this was." He spread his arms. "Fighting with Carlo and your erratic behavior made you the perfect suspect. So I hid until you found his body."

From the moment Leila linked Joshua to Robert Wynford, one detail had bothered her.

"Why would Charlotte provide you with an alibi?"

Orion had also not been able to figure out why the programming director would lie.

"Because I told her if she didn't, I'd tell Helen Cates about her attempt to get her off the Lincoln Center board. Her first strike was to take you off the concert which, unfortunately for her, failed." Joshua stepped forward. "I really was having dinner and drinks with her until I left to meet Carlo, so it was a matter of fudging the time by half an hour."

Nine to eleven PM were the busiest hours at Fionetto with post-concert crowds flooding the cafe for drinks and desserts. No one would've noticed the exact time Joshua slipped out.

Joshua took another step, his face darkening, loose gaze focused somewhere on Leila's forehead.

"In a few minutes, the concert will end," he said, his voice matching the music's *pianissimo*, "and your parents will walk in here and see the person they'd invested so much money in is gone."

Leila swallowed. "The cops know about you. They'll find you."

"That's okay." He smiled, gentle, reassuring. "You're a performer, Leila. Once you're gone, you're gone. This concert?" He nodded toward the speaker. "It's ephemeral, a momentary experience. Ten, twenty, fifty years from now, no one will be around to remember what happened. But I created something. My music will survive without me. Each time someone performs it for a new audience, it'll be reborn and live on."

The music faded away, leaving behind the sound of Leila's heart slamming against her ribs.

Applause boomed from the speakers.

Joshua raised the gun.

Leila lunged, the folds of her gown buffeting around her like a silk balloon, and shoved the scissors as hard as she could into the thigh of his injured leg.

A sound popped, sharp and crisp, above her head and Joshua let out a cry.

He fell back and Leila landed hard beside him, knee slamming against the tile, aching hand slick with sweat.

Beside her, the scissors protruded from Joshua's upper thigh, not large enough to cause significant injury.

Leila scrambled, stumbled over the hem of her skirt.

Joshua grunted and yanked her back.

Leila tumbled, lost in the silk, tripping over her heels, tangled in her costume. Joshua grabbed her shoulders and slammed her hard on her back.

Pain ricocheted up her spine and shoulders. Leila kicked, clawing at his jaw, his chest.

He hammered a fist into her shoulder and Leila cried out, her arm dropping uselessly to her side.

Breathing hard, Joshua climbed on top of her, his legs holding her wrists tight to her side, and sat on her stomach, paralyzing her diaphragm. The scissors were gone and blood seeped from the gash in a dark trickle.

Applause continued cascading from the speakers, a rhythmic roar of hunger.

Joshua locked his gloved hands around her neck and squeezed.

Leila's feet thrashed, her body howling for air, but she couldn't dislodge him.

Above her, shadows darkened Joshua's face, his eyes glittering pinpoints of zealous faith, lips curling with the rage of righteousness.

His thumbs dug into her throat and the crushing pressure increased.

Leila's vision flickered.

Never-ending applause wove in and out of the darkness hurtling toward her, a demanding cry she would never be able to satisfy…

Joshua's head snapped to the side.

A red mist punched through the side of his neck, showering Leila in crimson drops.

His mouth opened slightly, surprised, maybe a little sad, the echoes of his fanaticism still burning in his eyes.

He toppled over, landing hard beside her.

Leila coughed, sucked in air and blood, heard the frantic wheeze of her bruised throat and panicked lungs.

The applause finally stopped.

She touched her throat, felt the sticky drops spattered against her skin. Joshua's lifeless eyes gazed up at her, his blood already staining the silk hem of her crushed gown.

Some deaths were long, the decay so gradual the rotted end was nothing more than a sigh disappearing in the wind.

Others were quick, the abrupt cut of a life in mid-phrase leaving unanswered questions lingering like an unresolved harmony.

"Are you all right?"

Leila dragged her gaze away from Joshua.

Eyes the color of a snowy New York sky met hers.

Life, not death.

"How?" she croaked.

"I talked to Sayaka before the concert about the competition four years ago. She said you'd asked her about it, too, including questions about a student named Wynford. Ran his name through the system during intermission."

He showed her his phone. On the screen, an expired New York State driver's license for Robert Wynford displayed a photo of a slightly younger Joshua.

Leila dragged herself to the sofa and fell against it.

Orion exhaled, stood, and dialed.

He brought the phone to his ear, his tall frame blocking the speakers.

"I liked it," he said gruffly. "Your playing."

Leila closed her eyes, the echoes of Strauss and violence still vibrating in her chest.

She clenched her hands, wondering when, if ever, they'd stop trembling.

"Thanks."

TWELVE

V ladimir sat beside the window, the trickle of morning light
dipping into the wrinkled folds of his large hands.

He turned at the click of the door.

"Leila."

His gaze caught on the purple bruises marking her neck.

This was her first stop after a sleepless night of answering question after
question, repeating the same words to paramedics and doctors, to Brian
and the police.

Now she wanted to be answered.

The shelves lining the walls were filled with precious old scores, their
yellowed pages marked in Russian. Their crumbling spines greeted her
with the same fading sadness lingering around Vladimir.

He'd allowed his students to study those pages, absorb the notes left by
his legendary teacher.

Being in this studio had always made Leila feel as though she belonged
to a tradition far greater than her, something that kept her from floating
away in a sea of unceasing emptiness.

She belonged to art.

But today, she found no comfort.

The two Steinway pianos dominating the space no longer felt like
warm friends; now they appeared dull and overused, the keys pounded on
for years by faceless, forgotten students.

"You know," Vladimir said simply.

She joined him by the window. "Yes."

The tip of his bulbous nose flared red. He'd already dipped deep into his Thermos.

"Was it the only time my mother offered you something to help me?"

His silence was all the answer she needed.

Vladimir's stories about Russia, his stubborn declarations about art and music, the passionate exuberance with which he embraced music and life were all promises to Leila, vows that he would never be like her parents, a pledge to stand beside her as teacher and champion.

"Tell me."

Vladimir rubbed a hand over his face. "It is done."

"Please."

"Why bring up something —"

She touched his large hands. "Because that's the least you can do."

Vladimir dropped his head, shaggy dull hair covering his downcast eyes like a chastised dog.

"Helen came to me years ago. Wanted me to watch over you. Help you. She flew me out to hear you play in California." He waved his hand. "Recital. You played some Prokofiev, Debussy, Bach."

Leila remembered that performance, an exclusive dinner and reception at the home of one of her father's associates.

She didn't see or speak to Vladimir that night.

"Is that when you spoke with her about SMI?"

"No." He picked up his cup, took another long drink. "I told your mother I could not accept you as a student."

Something twisted inside Leila. "Why?"

"Because your playing…" Vladimir shook his head, his accent thickening. "You are the first pianist in the story, the one who sees your art through the world and not the other way around. I could not take you because you would die in this business —"

"But you did." Leila couldn't keep the accusation out of her voice. "You took me. You took her money."

"It was the last year of Larissa's life," he whispered. "Doctors and medicine were so expensive and I could do nothing to help her pain. Helen offered to take care of that. To pay for the best treatment American medicine could provide."

Leila turned away, leaned her aching shoulder against the window.

"Your mother was good to my wife, Leila. Please understand."

"But the competition was never about Larissa."

It had been about him, about resurrecting a career pissed away through vodka and self-pity, a desperate attempt to reclaim a time that no longer existed.

"You do not understand," he muttered.

"No, I don't."

"If an artist like Horowitz or Richter or Oistrakh played before the public now, do you think people would recognize what they heard, understand the level of it?" He spread his arms, eyes wide with indignation. "People are throwing money now at musicians who learn to plunk out a toy keyboard in six months and call them artistic geniuses."

He gestured toward the pianos in disgust. "Thirty-five years ago, my students asked me what it meant to become an artist. Besides music, they read books, studied art, understood film and dance and theater. Now, they ask me how to get a recording contract, how to become famous, how to market themselves and get an agent."

Vladimir stood, his shoulders hunched, his gaze flickering wildly across the pianos, the shelves of scores.

"Fast food, fast money, shallow thinking, shallow interpretations. This is now what I deal with everyday. Art was meant to be about freedom, about having the courage to explore what it means to be human. But now the people who control it have MBAs and no education in culture or humanities."

Vladimir strode over to the concert poster hanging against the far wall. It was from forty-five years ago during his debut European tour with the Concertgebouw Orchestra performing the Rachmaninoff Third.

A handsome, young, Vladimir leaned against the piano, his dark eyes containing a swagger that reminded Leila of Carlo.

"I played the world's greatest halls." Vladimir swayed. "A revelation, they called me! The star of the Soviet. Lines to buy tickets to my concert, standing ovations, the applause…" He swallowed. "The applause never stopped. I once played eight encores in one night. Chopin, Bach, Schumann, Rachmaninoff. Still, they wanted more."

He turned to her, eyes bright with evangelical belief, red nose burning like a flame. "Did you know George Soltano begged me to join his company? To come to America and bring my music here?"

Leila briefly closed her eyes and nodded.

"He flew me over first-class, picked me up at the airport in a limousine, and brought me to his office, directly across from Carnegie Hall. Back then, during the Cold War, I was a very young man and it left a huge impression on me. Do you know who took my suitcases out of the limousine? Carried them up for me to the office? His daughter."

Leila slumped against the window, her chest aching in the same way it did when she found out Sayaka had also entered the competition, that her friend had also once silently dreamed of something more.

"Marlene was in high school. A complete mess." Vladimir waved his hand. "Behaved more like his ex-wife than like George. It was summer and George wanted her to gain experience and be serious about her life. He had her follow and care for some of the world's greatest artists so she could learn about work and music."

The fervent rage dissipated, his expression adopting a fragility very much at odds with his large, hulking figure.

"But George always knew she didn't have his gift. Marlene was spoiled, entitled. Didn't know the difference between Brahms or Bach, between Stravinsky and Schumann. Do you understand now, Leila?"

She did, but she was too sad and weary to answer.

He looked at her, his eyes dark holes of broken despair.

"She carried my suitcases and now she decides if I am allowed to play."

****

Light glowed beneath the large door at the east end of the floor. The other offices were empty this late in the evening.

Leila knocked.

"Come in."

Marlene sat behind a glass desk with her legs crossed, the black leather chair swallowing her slim figure. Behind her, a large window revealed a breathtaking display of midtown including the bright lights of Carnegie.

Marlene followed her gaze. "Nice, isn't it?"

"It is." Leila took a seat.

"The Berlin Phil is playing tonight."

"I heard them last night. The Schubert was astounding."

A pause. "You moved out of your home."

"Yes."

Marlene studied her, but didn't press further.

Leila had never been interested in promotion and publicity. Interviews and articles only increased the pressure she felt before a performance so she'd learned long ago to simply not read them.

But she'd become fascinated with the demise of her career.

Peter Foerstner's article - published two days after Joshua's rage nearly choked the life out of her - had captured every sordid detail of her life and magnified it.

Carlo's lovers, all hungry, ambitious musicians, had come forward eager to finally have their names linked with the dead maestro.

As expected, the depiction of Carlo had been one of admiration, glorifying his talent and emphasizing the tragedy of its loss.

Carlo Belandini: The Legacy Collection, a special edition of all his recordings, would release in a few months.

The most damning parts of the article had been reserved for Helen, Paul, and Leila Cates.

Helen's actions over the years were laid out in exquisite detail: her coercion of Vladimir Markov to get Leila into Juilliard, her manipulation of the conservatory's competition. There were also details of at least three major competitions in which Helen Cates (and Paul by association) clearly had a hand.

Foerstner had gambled and won. The story had become the most e-mailed article in the *New York Times* with over two thousand comments and no golf or dinner dates with Paul Cates could delete its impact.

Columbia University had cancelled the new performing hall's dedication ceremony, citing event complications. Due to contractual obligations, the hall would still retain the Cates name.

Several musicians, who'd lost to Leila in previous competitions, came forward to file legal action suit against the Cates and Brian Kensington had gleefully accepted a healthy retainer to deal with them.

Leila had not spoken to her parents in the two weeks since the story broke.

After returning from Vladimir's studio, she'd cut up her credit cards, packed, and left that mausoleum of an apartment to find her life.

She'd moved into a temporary room in Queens with two suitcases, one filled entirely with her scores. The only money she had left was the fee she'd received for her Lincoln Center debut.

Marlene looked at her. "Most of the company doesn't want you on the roster."

Leila nodded.

The scandal was enough to permanently tarnish her career. No one wanted to hire someone who'd cheated their way to the top, someone whose actions had resulted in robbing the world of a real artist like Carlo Belandini.

It didn't matter how she played.

Leila doubted it ever had.

"You can't spin this."

Marlene leaned back and narrowed her eyes. The city glittered behind her, avaricious and all-knowing.

"No one wants to touch you. You're too much of a risk."

Heinrich and Elliot remained on Juilliard's faculty. Heinrich's powerful position in Germany and Elliot's undeniable star power meant it wasn't in the school's best interests to let go of either one.

But Vladimir had left. According to the school's PR department, it was on amicable terms.

Marlene alone had somehow escaped the scandal unscathed. Peter Foerstner made no mention of her in his article and Leila wondered what bargain Marlene had struck to ensure none of this touched her.

"Is Helen still paying you a retainer?" Leila asked stiffly.

Marlene uncrossed her legs. "No."

"Then why are you keeping me?"

Marlene picked up a pen, tapped the edge of the table, and behind the hard sheen in her eyes, Leila saw a hint of that wild teenager Vladimir remembered, the person who despised structure and eased her loneliness in the bed of a man half her age.

"Because I want to see what you do now."

Leila's hands reflexively arched in her lap. "I need work."

"No solos."

Leila gave a stiff nod. "What did you have in mind?"

The office landline beeped. Marlene buzzed someone in.

"We'll have to wait a little until things cool down," she said. "But next season, I think we might be able to put you somewhere."

Eight months of no concerts. Leila did some fast calculations. What she had in her bank account would last her two months at the most.

"I have a large repertoire," Leila said. "If there's somewhere I can substitute or fill in —"

A knock came at the door.

"Come in."

The door opened and a stunningly beautiful woman entered.

Natalie Arena exuded a powerful mix of cool confidence and seductive mysteriousness. The foremost concert violinist in the world, with over a hundred tour dates across the globe each year, she had the career of Leila's dreams.

Graceful, elegant, and commanding a sophisticated artistry full of finesse and passion, Natalie Arena was the epitome of a superstar.

"You must be Leila." A slight mediterranean accent colored her voice.

She took her hand and Leila let her.

"You'll play with Natalie on her European recital tour in the fall," Marlene said.

"You mean accompany her?" Leila blinked. "But I…that's not what I do."

Natalie dropped her hand, looked at Marlene with a quizzical expression.

Leila had imagined she'd play chamber music, maybe trios or quintets with some of the roster's other soloists, an exciting intersection of personalities and talents.

But accompanying Natalie wasn't chamber music.

This was about being relegated to the very bottom, becoming a superfluous non-entity whose only purpose was to follow the person on stage.

Marlene's flat eyes grew colder. "Would you like me to give it to someone else?"

"No." Leila swallowed her pride. "No, of course not. I'd be happy to do it."

"I have listened to your recordings, Leila. You are a wonderful pianist and I can't wait to work with you." Natalie touched her shoulder and Leila felt her pity. "We are women. We will make good music together."

This was temporary, the first step in finding her way again.

Tread. Stay afloat.

Leila smiled. "Absolutely."

Natalie leaned in and pressed a quick kiss to both cheeks.

Her perfume wafted over Leila, a cloud of privilege and whispered promises entwined with the distinct scent of overripe fruit.

ACKNOWLEDGMENTS

Thank you to my husband and family for their unflagging support and for accommodating my unusual schedule.

To Maya, Lara, Aaron, Katya, Brian, David, Alex, and Jeff: thank you and I miss you.

Thanks to IA, FD, JA, and BT for cheering me on and to Sasha, Sam, Javi, Blake, and Cathy for their feedback and wisdom. Much gratitude to my cover designer, Grady at Damonza, for the fabulous artwork. Many thanks also to my editor, Bryon Quertermous, for guiding me through and to my assistant, Jan Lewis, for keeping me on track.

To the Elites: Sarah Amer, Tricia Ballard, Samantha Cunningham, Jennifer Desantis, Melanie Hall, Vicky Robb, Jacqueline Mellow, Grace Touma, Tessa Unruh, Heather Villalvazo, Lindsay Weber, and Aziza Yogore. Your encouragement, warmth, and sincerity always brighten my day and I remain ever grateful that I've been fortunate enough to share this journey with you.

And as always, my very deepest thanks to my readers. I couldn't do this without you.

A WOVEN SILENCE

In a small, forgotten town at the foothills of Blue Mountain, three children decide to take the future into their hands, changing the course of their lives forever...

Despite the unraveling of her personal life, concert pianist Leila Cates returns to a world she thought she'd left behind and is pulled into a murder investigation that stretches from New York's glittering stages to the belly of the criminal underworld.

Leila teams up again with NYPD Detective Orion Frazier and what begins with the death of a prominent businessman quickly turns into a twisted maze of deception and betrayal.

Struggling with a violence spanning over two decades, Leila and Orion discover long-buried secrets that set off a dangerous chain of events. How far would people go to protect those they love?

An unnerving psychological thriller, *A Woven Silence* is a riveting novel of love and loyalty, retribution and atonement, in which four individuals confront their darkest truths and a past that will not die.

Subscribe to Emma Raveling's newsletter to receive new release announcements!

www.emmaraveling.com

ABOUT THE AUTHOR

Emma Raveling writes a wide variety of fiction for teens and adults. She is the author of the young adult urban / contemporary fantasy series, the Ondine Quartet, and the adult suspense thrillers, *Breaking Measures* and *A Woven Silence*.

An avid traveler, she currently resides in Honolulu with her husband and German shepherd.

Website: emmaraveling.com
Twitter: @emmaraveling
Facebook: /emmaraveling
Instagram: @emmaraveling

www.ingramcontent.com/pod-product-compliance
Lightning Source LLC
Chambersburg PA
CBHW021156130626
46554CB00005B/1848